RAVEN LYNNE

What Really Happened

A Tactical Suspense Romance Novel

RAVEN
RISING
BOOKS

First published by Raven Rising Books 2025

Library of Congress Control Number: 2025917642 (hardcover) 2025915990 (paperback)

Disclaimer:

First edition

ISBN (paperback): 979-8-9990673-1-9
ISBN (hardcover): 979-8-9990673-2-6

This book was professionally typeset on Reedsy.
Find out more at reedsy.com

To my mom, who always wanted me to be a writer. I finally had a story worth sharing. And to my husband for being so supportive and patient with me as I drove myself crazy getting this book to the finish line.
And to the readers, who will notice every typo and run-on sentence, of a self-published and self-edited book, and still fall in love with these characters.
Thank you.

Authors Note

I've spent years working behind the scenes in criminal justice-related fields. My background includes a Master's degree in Administration of Justice with a concentration in criminal behavior, experience as a 911 dispatcher, and deep involvement in the self-defense training world. I've seen firsthand how preparedness, awareness, and calm under pressure can change outcomes and sometimes save lives.

That's what inspired What Really Happened.

This isn't just a mystery. It's a story that weaves practical, real-world training and safety principles into fiction. My goal is to make those lessons accessible, not by lecturing, but by immersing you in a narrative that's emotionally grounded and true to the challenges real people face. While the characters and plot are fictional, the risks they face reflect reality. Whether you're here for the slow-burn romance, the investigative twists, or the survival mindset, I hope this story keeps you turning pages, and maybe leaves you just a little more prepared to face the world.

Thank you for reading and for supporting independent authors who believe fiction can be both empowering and entertaining.

Content Note:

This book covers several heavy themes and is intended for adult readers. And uses adult language. While it doesn't get more graphic than a typical episode of Law & Order: SVU, it includes references to child sex crimes, human trafficking, and adult sexual content. Because this is a slow-burn romance, the authors reserved the intimate material mostly for the end of chapter 19, the final chapter before the epilogue (which readers may skip).

— Raven

Prologue

April 19th, 2019

Diana walked to her car with a bounce in her step. Today marked the start of a fresh chapter as an insurance claims adjuster.

She pulled out her phone to call her mom and let her know how it went, and noticed there were sixty-nine missed calls.

"What the fuck?" she muttered to herself.

Then her phone rang again.

"Hello?"

"Ma'am, this is Dr. Layton at Grand Strand Medical Center. EMS brought your mother in for a stroke."

Diana felt her world go sideways. She stumbled into her car and sat down.

"What?" she choked out.

"She's stable, but we don't know how long ago the symptoms started," he advised.

"Jesus," Diana groaned, her mind racing. That was bad. Getting to the hospital quickly was critical during strokes. She talked to Mom last night, and she'd been fine then.

"Grand Strand? What room?" she managed.

"She's being admitted. Check in with the front desk to see if they've moved her when you arrive. I'll be on hand to give you a full report."

"Thank you. I'm coming from Pawleys Island, so it'll be a bit."

Facts first. Panic later, she told herself. She threw her Camry into drive and peeled out of the parking lot.

Her thoughts were racing about what to do. Reagan... she should tell Reagan. It was spring break. Perhaps her niece could escape her vicious mother for a few days and visit. That would mean the world to her mom.

Hell, it would mean the world to her. Because... she didn't really have any other family to call.

She hit the speed dial on her car's screen.

"Ring... ring... ring..." No answer.

She tried again.

"RING... RING... RING..." Still no answer.

"Answer the phone, REAGAN!" she yelled at her dashboard. Her thoughts continued to spiral. For a fifteen-year-old content creator who lived on her phone, not answering was incredibly weird.

Okay... who could she call that was local, and would actually care?

She thought of her mom's friends, then immediately dismissed the idea. Old busybodies. All of them. Not until she knew more.

Traci. Her best friend. She might still be at work at the restaurant, but she'd take it personally if Diana didn't call her.

"Ring.. ring... ring. Hey girl, hey! How was your first day?" Traci answered brightly.

"Mom's in the hospital. I'm hauling ass to Grand Strand right now. She's had a stroke."

"Oh, my god. Really?"

"Yeah. They said she's stable, thank God, but they don't know how long ago the symptoms started. So that's making me think there's a high possibility for brain damage."

"Oh my god, I'm so sorry. Let me come meet you up there."

"No, it's okay. I know you're busy at work with the spring breakers. I'll keep you posted, though."

"Fuck the spring breakers. You don't always have to do everything alone, Diana," Traci snapped.

"I'm not alone. I'm gonna get Reagan to come," Diana said, hoping it was true.

Traci let out a deep sigh. "Fine... keep me posted. But I will see you up there at the end of my shift."

Diana arrived at the hospital after calling Reagan fifteen more times. Still no answer.

"I'm Diana Ramsey. I'm here to see my mom, Vickie Ramsey. They said she was being admitted," she told the security guard. The familiar smell of the hospital brought back too many memories. She pushed them away to focus on the present.

They directed her to the ICU. She walked into the room, her stomach in knots. Her mom looked pale and frail as she lay unconscious in the hospital bed.

The nurse sent for the doctor, who arrived with a somber expression.

His words hit like concrete.

"She is stable and responding well. The major concern is whether there was brain damage. We'll be looking to see if coordination and speech are affected, and if they are, rehab will hopefully help her regain what may be lost. We won't really know more till she wakes up. But you should start making arrangements for her to be in long-term care."

As he left, the nurse returned with questions about current medications and any allergies her mom may have. But Diana wasn't sure. Other than being allergic to bee stings, her mom was as healthy as a horse as far as she knew.

A case manager also stopped by to introduce themselves and go over what type of care options were available in the community.

The flood of information hit her like a tidal wave. Diana rushed to the bathroom and threw up.

She had watched her mom go through all of this before. First with her dad, then, when her brother Jacob died. Now, it all fell to her.

Figuring out the insurance, bills, the house, and her mom's care, it was going to feel like a full-time job on top of her actual full-time job.

The life she thought she was building, full of travel, independence, and a promising new career, was slipping through her fingers.

Then came the guilt. How could she be thinking about her job at a time like this? Mom was still alive. That's what mattered.

She forced herself to focus on what needed to happen next: Get ahold of Reagan.

As much as she hated talking to Layla, it was time to call and find out why Reagan wasn't answering.

"Ring ring ring, DIANA!" Layla screamed into the phone.

The noise shocked her.

"LAYLA!" Diana screamed back. She was being a little petty, sure, but if her ears had to suffer, so did Layla's.

"Where's Reagan?" they both asked in unison.

"I don't know," Layla said.

"What do you mean, you don't know?" Diana's anger surged. This woman. This trashy, chaotic mess her brother had somehow loved enough to marry was always like this.

"Diana... Reagan's missing. I think she ran away."

5 Years Later

"She vanished, and they labeled her a runaway. But I've seen the timeline. And I'm telling you, it doesn't add up.

Welcome to Second Look Cases. I'm your host, Sam Benson. Today, we're looking at a case that desperately needs a second look.

Shout-out to Tasha, my neighbor's kid, for dragging this one back into the light. If the name Reagan Ramsey sounds familiar. It should.

She was internet-famous before the term "influencer" was even a thing. Six years old, unboxing toys in plastic tiaras. Fighting make-believe dragons for millions of views. She was a hit with kids everywhere.

But as she got older, so did the content. Every awkward phase, every bad haircut, every fight with her mom, was public.

Then one day? She was just... gone. Her mom says she emptied her accounts and ran. And for a while, people believed that.

That was five years ago. No phone calls. No verified sightings. No trace.

But lately? That narrative's cracking. People from her past are finally talking. Stuff that made little sense before is lining up in ways that give me chills.

And the more I dig, the more this feels less like a teenage rebellion and more like someone is pulling strings to cover up the truth.

So let's do what no one else has. Let's look closer. Let's question everyone.

And let's find out what really happened to Reagan Ramsey?"

Chapter 1

Diana looked at the calendar. April 11th, 2024.

Next week would mark five years since her niece Reagan went missing.

A familiar ache welled in her chest as the light glinted off a golden frame perched on the edge of her desk. Drawing her eyes to the last photo they'd taken together. A small snapshot of a time that now felt impossibly distant.

For one week each summer, Reagan's mom, Layla, would let her come to South Carolina to spend time with this side of the family.

A brief escape from the cameras and the constant content creation in L.A., Reagan was a brand there. In Pawleys Island, she got to be a kid.

Diana had always thought of those visits as a kind of rescue, a chance to breathe.

Pawleys was full of retirees who didn't even know what YouTube was. Reagan could go out in public, laugh too loud, wear mismatched pajamas to the store, and no one cared.

"I should've done more," Diana whispered to herself.

But the logical part of her mind pushed back. She had been caring for her mother, who suffered severe aphasia after a stroke.

Every day had been a relentless game of charades, trying to guess what her mom needed: food, water, or pain meds?

Now, Mom was gone too. Another stroke had taken her six months ago. And the house was too quiet without her.

Focus, she told herself, straightening in her chair. There was work to do.

She went back to looking through the security camera footage of the beachfront bar that had burned down. Making sure there was no evidence of arson. The insurance company she worked for had no reason to suspect that there would be. However, an investigation still had to be made.

A dark figure stumbled into the frame of the camera. He appeared to be smoking with the gestures of periodic movements towards his mouth. He made his way to the back of the building, then darted away.

Moments later, flames engulfed the tall grass, and Diana noted the timestamp and the suspect's direction of travel. We have our source. Now we need an identity.

A different camera angle showed the dark figure getting into a car. Diana could make out that it was a Tesla. But not the license plate. Luckily, there weren't many people who owned Teslas in this town. Coincidentally, the owner of the bar was one of them.

She had to hand it to the guy. Burning down his business across the street from the local insurance agency building was ballsy. Or, the dumbass thought that because he'd been friends with the broker since high school, he'd be able to protect him from the consequences.

"Hate to burst your bubble, dude, but you're gonna go to jail. Do not pass go, do not collect $200." Diana said out loud to herself with a touch of dark humor to lighten the darkness of her thoughts.

Being able to work from home had really helped her take care of her mom when she was alive. It also gave her the habit of talking to herself out loud a lot.

She dialed the police detective assigned to this case.

"Hey, Detective Ray, how are you today?" She said in greeting.

"What do you have this time?" He asked. His tone was a little short.

"Arson, your favorite."

He responded gruffly. "Shit, for real?"

"Yeah. We have the cameras at the insurance brokerage across the street from Beachwoods. You can clearly see someone setting the fire and then getting into a Tesla."

"You're fucking kidding me. I tried to get those tapes, and the receptionist said the cameras weren't working."

"They were. They're actually saved on a cloud server provided by corporate.

So...you're welcome. I'll email you the clip."

"Thanks. I owe you one."

Diana snorted.

"You owe me like 12. I introduced you to your wife. But I'll talk at you later."

Detective Ray had been good friends with her brother, Jacob. They were ten years older than her. When Jacob had died, Ray had taken the time to stay close to the family. Even now, they were still close friends.

Jacob died in a training accident on an Army helicopter just weeks before Reagan was born. His funeral had been the first time they'd met Layla.

Their whirlwind romance, marriage, and pregnancy had all happened very fast, and although at that first meeting, everything had seemed normal. When Diana and Vickie arrived to meet baby Reagan, they realized what kind of person Jacob had married and were horrified.

Layla was rude, entitled, and demanding. Diana was pretty sure she made one aide cry who didn't move fast enough to suit her. But silent they remained.

Empathizing with how Layla must feel. One month burying her husband and the next giving birth to a child, she was going to be raising on her own.

Now she knew how correct those first impressions had been. Hindsight, after all, was 20/20.

Her phone rang. She looked down, figuring it would be Detective Ray calling her back for something, but it was an unknown number.

"Hello?"

"Hi, is this Diana Ramsey?"

"Sure is," she responded.

"Hi, my name is Sam Benson..." he trailed off like that was supposed to be easily recognizable. He continued after a long, awkward pause.

"I have the investigative podcast, Second Look Cases. Have you heard of it?"

"Not really my thing. How can I help you?"

"Oh, well," he sounded a little deflated. Diana waited for him to get to the point.

"We are doing a story about your niece, Reagan Ramsey. Have you had any contact with her since she went missing 5 years ago?"

Shock crashed into her. She couldn't help but glance at the photo on the edge of her desk. She gripped the phone tightly and took a deep breath to steady her voice before answering.

"No, last time I talked to her mom, Layla, she said she'd run away and took all the money and was likely on a yacht sailing around the world."

"And you believe that?" He asked.

Dammit, he must have heard the suspicion in the family tagline. Layla and her lawyers had told them to use it to keep the media frenzy at bay when Reagan first disappeared.

"It didn't really matter if I believed it or not. Layla is Reagan's mom. Why aren't you calling her?"

"You haven't heard?" He asked.

"Heard what?"

"Layla Ramsey died two months ago from a drug overdose."

"Of course she did," Diana responded before she realized she shouldn't have said that.

There was an awkward pause, and it seemed her lack of filter had surprised him.

"Listen. I want to interview you if that's okay. I want to go back and reopen Reagan's case with fresh eyes because I want to find her and bring her home."

Tears blurred Diana's vision before she could blink them away. She'd just been thinking the same thing, that she should've done more. The guilt hit like a punch to the ribs.

She'd handed everything over to Layla, thinking it was the logical choice. Layla was Reagan's mother, after all. The family's public face. But now all she could think about was *how wrong had she been?*

That gnawing suspicion in her gut, the one she'd ignored for years, was now impossible to quiet. He was right to ask questions about Layla. Diana had always felt something was off, but she'd never dared to say it out loud. Saying it would make it real. And that was too horrible to believe.

The hope that Reagan might show up one day, with some dramatic, maybe even apologetic excuse for why she'd run, was fading fast.

Diana swallowed hard and spoke, her voice cracking just enough to betray the storm inside.

"Of course, I want to bring her home. She knew she always had a home with me. That's why... when she ran away and didn't come here, I thought maybe she was mad at me, too. I thought she'd show up when she was ready."

"Let me show you what I've found, and do the interview, and then we can start trying to get the ball rolling on, warming up her cold case."

The term 'cold case' shot daggers into her heart. But he was right, after all this time...cold cases like Reagan's usually only had one outcome, if any closure at all.

Diana hesitated. Doing interviews was not something she had ever prepared for. She had been just far removed enough from the spotlight that no one had ever asked her about Reagan in an official capacity like this.

Her mom had gotten a few phone calls, but other than telling the reporters and investigators that her mom had a stroke and she could no longer communicate. No one had asked them about Reagan in years.

"Okay. Show me what you got, and then I'll decide if I want to do an interview."

"I'm sorry, that's not how this works. See, as a content creator, I am going to need to capture your authentic reaction, or else I'm out of business."

"Seriously?" She groaned.

"I'm afraid so. I do really want to help, but I also enjoy being able to pay my bills. It can get tricky sometimes." He sounded almost apologetic.

"Yeah, profiting off other people's misery sounds tricky."

"I figured you working in insurance would understand," He clapped back. Diana would be impressed if not for the dread she was feeling at agreeing to this, but she could see the connection. Working for an insurance company, people typically thought you had no soul.

"Whatever, dude. So, how do you want to do this?" She asked.

"I can meet you at your house tomorrow, around 4 pm. It'll be me, my producer, and our camera guy. I'll need something like a kitchen table to lay the evidence out on. Other than that, it'll be just a normal conversation with me. The goal is to go over what we thought we knew and what we know now."

Diana had a million different thoughts and emotions racing through her head, but at least she had about twenty-four hours to prepare.

She was a little suspicious of this guy and the whole situation. As she glanced again at the picture of Reagan. A powerful urge to do something had her saying,

"Ok, I'll see you then," before she could think any better of it.

Chapter 2

Diana spent the night researching this Sam Benson guy. She found a lot of information that others probably couldn't because of her ties in insurance.

He'd been an investigative reporter for the Washington Post who was fired for breaking a story on Capitol Hill about elected officials having swinger parties. He'd included the name of the Post's owner on the list of attendees.

It caused the owner to get a very expensive and messy divorce. But that story gave Sam Benson a cult-like following for being a truth seeker. He should have been able to get another job somewhere else, but he went independent and started a podcast instead. Probably, so he no longer had to answer to anyone. Diana thought.

He was harsh to some people he interviewed, pushing them with questions no one else would dare ask. He would have moments of compassion with others. Diana had the feeling it was all manufactured to present the story in the way he wanted to fit his narrative.

He often said in interviews that he had no filter because filters blocked the truth. Diana suspected it was less about honesty and more about ego. Just an excuse to be rude and call it noble. Watching him in those clips, she saw the same smug half-smile, the boyish glint in his eye when he caught someone off-guard. He reminded her of the guys in college who got away with too much charm and too few consequences.

Charming, yes, but also immature. Unfiltered didn't always mean honest. Sometimes it just meant undisciplined.

He had only just started this podcast about two years ago. His first big case was about Missing and Murdered Indigenous Women, commonly referred to as MMIW, she learned. That case had taken him on the road for months. Sharing stories that mainstream media had missed for years, and it had catapulted him to podcast fame.

The trick would be not to fall into any of the emotional traps. The guy had really sharp instincts and wasn't afraid to apply pressure to get the answers he was looking for.

He would probably use her insecurity, that she felt guilty that she didn't do enough against her. Possibly blowing every comment she made out of proportion. Or twist the sense of humor she was famous for into making her look bad. Something she didn't have the energy to deal with. But Diana would be ready for that, and would try to keep the interview from becoming a hit piece about her niece or her family.

It had been uncharacteristically cold that week, so Diana opted for a long-sleeve black turtleneck and leggings. The only adornment was a delicate gold heart necklace.

She and Reagan had picked out matching ones the last time she'd visited, and it felt right to wear hers today.

Reagan had loved shopping, especially the little touristy spots along the Grand Strand. She used to say they were her favorite because it was never about brands or sponsorships, just vibes.

The knock at the door came five minutes early.

She opened the door, and it wasn't Sam who was knocking. It was a middle-aged, slightly pudgy man with a balding head, glasses, and a graying goatee.

Diana looked at him with confusion, her hand hovering over the hem of her shirt, just in case she needed to draw the gun she had concealed. It would be just her luck that this was all a scam. Then she saw Sam walking up to the house, and relief washed through her.

"Thank you for doing this, Diana," He called out as she made way for what had to be his producer, the pudgy man. As she saw a younger, athletic black guy behind Sam, carrying what had to be the camera equipment.

"This is Brent Humboldt." Sam said, pointing to the producer, "And this is DeMarcus Jackson." He said, pointing to the camera guy. "And I am, of course, Sam." He said, holding his hand out for a handshake as she closed the door behind them.

He was a tall, classically good-looking guy with black hair and piercing blue eyes. He was probably about her age, with a chiseled jaw and broad shoulders. The epitome of tall, dark, and handsome.

After her deep dive into researching him, she'd expected someone intelligent and ruthless. Sam certainly fit the bill. He also clearly knew the effect he had on women.

What she hadn't prepared for was the spark of attraction she felt.

He had the eyes of a hunter. His polite smile as he shook her hand did nothing to lessen the intensity of focus, and she noticed that her hand tingled as he released it.

She crushed the feeling instantly and looked away. Then led them down the hallway to the living area, reminding herself of exactly why they were here.

Still, she couldn't stop the hairs on the back of her neck from rising, acutely aware of him walking behind her.

Diana's small townhouse didn't have a formal dining room. Just an island with bar seating and a living room with a giant coffee table. So that is where she showed them to set up.

Moving here had been a blessing when her mom got sick. Having the HOA take care of the yard maintenance had given her less to have to worry about.

Her mom had the downstairs bedroom while she had an office in the upstairs landing, and her bedroom up there had given her enough separation and privacy over the years that she could still feel like an adult.

"Would y'all like anything to drink before we get started?" Diana asked as DeMarcus set up the camera next to the TV.

"Sure, I would love some water," Sam said with a small smile. It reminded Diana of a book she read once that said to think of charming as a verb, not an adjective. He was trying to be nice and polite and lure her into a false sense of security.

Her instincts warned her not to fall for it. Interviewing people was her favorite part of the job, and she'd studied his style enough to be ready.

He probably underestimated how much she'd learned about him. She planned to keep it that way for as long as she needed to see what his angle was.

Brent dragged one of her barstools over to the coffee table, creating a clear degree of separation. She knew then he wasn't planning to play nice.

Diana pulled down the water glasses and filled them, handing them out to the team.

"One more thing, for clear audio. We'll need you to wear this lapel mic," Sam said, holding it up.

DeMarcus was still tangled in gear, clearly searching for something. Sam glanced at Diana's outfit and frowned.

"Turtlenecks are a bit of a problem…"

"No worries," she said, already heading toward the coat closet. "I've got a blazer that'll work."

She returned a moment later, slipping into the black blazer with practiced ease.

Sam stepped toward her. He lifted her long red hair gently off her shoulder, then clipped the mic to her lapel. His hands were steady, professional, and a little warm.

"Turn around?" he asked.

She did, and that's when he saw it.

"What's this?"

"Corset holster."

"Holster?" he lowered his voice, eyes narrowing. "You're armed?"

"I mean… a group of strange men were coming to my house," she said over her shoulder. "Of course I'm armed."

He paused, then gave a single, amused nod. "Fair. Totally fair. Just let me get this mic pack on and we'll get started."

Once he finished, he waved to DeMarcus. "Sound check?"

DeMarcus gave a thumbs-up.

And they took their positions in the living room.

Sam had a folder full of papers on his lap, which Diana assumed was the evidence he was hoping to get a reaction to.

DeMarcus was in the living room corner by the TV, and Brent hovered in the hallway, just out of sight of the camera, and started counting down to when the filming would begin.

Diana had the photo of Mom, Reagan, and herself from the beach waiting for her on the coffee table. She picked it up to hold it in her lap. Unsure of what to do with her hands.

She felt nervous. A wary anticipation. Like she was going into battle with an equally matched foe.

They'd barely said more than a few words so far, by Sam's design. He wanted the full reaction. Raw. On camera. She understood the tactic. But she was smart enough not to trust him.

She knew there was a good chance he would see through her armor of sarcastic humor and polite professionalism. That he would see that her heart was bleeding at the idea that she had failed Reagan, and twist all of those emotions to have her cry on camera for his viewers to gawk over.

Sam's voice broke the silence.

"For the record, can you give us your name and your relationship with Reagan Ramsey?"

His tone was calm.

Diana took a deep breath. Show time, she thought.

"I am Diana Ramsey," she said clearly. "Reagan is my niece. My brother Jacob was her father."

"Now Jacob died before she was born. Are you sure he was the father?"

Diana's eyes flew wide at the one question she hadn't expected. She set the picture down on the coffee table. Giving herself a moment to not say the first thing that came to her mind, which was fuck you for even suggesting such a thing.

Remembering all the times Reagan had reminded her and her mother of Jacob with the same dark hair, freckles, and mischievous grin.

It was something that was said often after her visits, that it was like having his mini-me here.

"I never had a doubt about that." She responded flatly. She decided not to elaborate.

"But you did have doubts about something?" He countered.

"Mr. Benson, I'm an Insurance Claims Adjuster. I have doubts in just about everything," she responded sarcastically.

He made no reaction, but there was a gleam in his eyes that Diana didn't trust.

"Were there doubts about Layla Ramsey?"

"Can you be more specific?"

"Was she a good mother?"

"I really wouldn't know. They lived in L.A. I live in South Carolina. I didn't even get to meet her until Jacob's funeral, and then when Reagan was born and maybe a handful of times after that."

"What caused the strained relationship that meant you didn't get to know her?" He persisted, clearly looking for a hook.

"Nothing, I was 16 when Reagan was born, I went to college, and about the time I graduated, she had started the internet thing and was busy. We tried to be supportive, and she would come every summer for a week. Typically, over Father's Day, to visit with my mom and our side of the family, that's all we got with Reagan."

"Ok, so you knew Layla was a stripper, and that your brother married her when she got pregnant with Reagan?" He asked. His focus was intent on the reaction to his words.

"Excuse me?" Diana blurted out. She could not hide the shock on her face. He continued.

"Yes, we looked into Layla's background, and it looks like she had been working at a strip club outside of Fort Campbell. That's where she met your brother, Jacob. We talked to guys stationed with him there, and apparently, that had been a big reason for him not bringing her home to meet the family before he died."

"I did not know," Diana said with her arms crossed in a defensive, if not defiant, way.

Sam noticed his approach wasn't working and changed track.

"Being 16 at the time may have had something to do with that."

"Probably." She responded.

There was a long, awkward pause that she filled by taking a sip of water while he adjusted himself on the stool.

"So let's change gears. Tell me about how you heard Reagan was missing."

"Well, it was the Friday I had just started working for the company I do now as a claims adjuster. I remember that. I didn't find out about it till later, because the phone call I got was that my mom had been rushed to the hospital because of a stroke."

"That happened the same day?" He looked perplexed.

"Yeah." Diana nodded. "I think she had found out, and the shock caused her to stroke out."

She took a deep breath before continuing. "After I got to the hospital and gotten a report from the doctor about her condition. I called friends and family to let them know what was going on. So when I couldn't get a hold of Reagan, I called Layla, and that's how I heard Reagan was missing."

She was proud of that response. She hadn't started crying.

"How much of the conversation with Layla do you remember?" He asked softly.

"Every damn word. Honestly."

He made a motion to continue. He was clearly on the edge of his seat for the retelling of that story.

"She told me Reagan was missing. Of course, I was shocked, and then she almost immediately started complaining about the money Reagan took."

"What did you say next?" He asked.

"Is cussing allowed? I probably should have asked about that before we got started." Diana said as she glanced at the camera. DeMarcus and Brent had really faded into the background while she'd been talking with Sam.

Sam gave a small nod and an almost grin.

"That obviously pissed me off, so I *laid* into Layla," Diana said, stressing the fact that she let the woman have it with both barrels.

"So I remember saying something along the lines of, Listen here bitch. That is my niece, and it's her fucking money, and she can do whatever she wants to with it. I am praying she files for emancipation to get away from your crazy ass. And I will do everything I can to help her." Diana said.

The remembered emotions from that conversation rose within her like ghosts from a grave.

"But you didn't help her?" He said, directly cutting through those feelings and shining a light on her greatest regret.

"I didn't know how to." She said almost automatically. "I called her a million times, messaged her on every social media platform. But I couldn't go to LA and turn over every stone; I had to take care of my mom. I also had to work; I had just started this job. I didn't have PTO. Plus, according to all of Layla's social media, she was taking care of everything. She'd called the cops, hired a private investigator, and printed out posters. Fuck, she even had billboards. What more could I have done?"

These were the words her friend Traci had often used whenever Diana mentioned to her how guilty she felt. They never stopped her from feeling guilty, but it seemed the best explanation she could give to try to convey how torn she'd been.

Sam paused, giving her a long look. Diana couldn't quite make out what his expression was supposed to be. But then Sam opened the folder. He handed Diana the first piece of paper.

"Have you seen this before?"

Diana's heart started beating wildly as she took in what he'd just handed her.

"No."

"Can you describe to the audience what this is?"

"It's a police report," she said. "She... tried to commit suicide?"

Tears spilled down Diana's face. She looked up at Sam, but he was still unreadable.

"What's the date on this report?" He asked for the audience's sake.

"October 15th." Diana read off.

"So... six months before she disappeared? Did you know about this?"

"No. I didn't." She shook her head.

He gave her a moment to read the full document.

"She took a bunch of pills?" Diana asked, with shaking hands.

Sam nodded.

"Oh god. What the hell was going on? I thought she was... mostly.. happy."

"She said nothing to you about her life in L.A.?" he asked, brow furrowing slightly.

"No. When she came to visit, we wanted her to get away from all that. We just focused on having fun. Letting her be a normal kid."

She looked up sharply. "How did you get this?"

"It was mentioned during the police press conference. A leak that was dismissed quickly."

"What did they say about it?"

"You didn't watch the press conference?"

She paused, trying to remember. Why would she have missed something that big? Then it hit her. "That was the day my mom got discharged from the hospital after her stroke."

Everything had been chaos.

She'd spent hours driving back and forth to Grand Strand Medical Center. It was an hour each way from her house in Pawleys.

The hospital had promised to send the equipment her mom needed home with her. They didn't. She spent the whole day on the phone with the case manager, desperately trying to make it work.

"I had it playing in the background," she added softly. "But I couldn't focus. I missed most of it. That day was hell."

Sam's expression shifted, just slightly, but she caught it.

A flicker of empathy.

"Was this the only time this came up?" she asked, dreading the answer.

"To my knowledge, yes. Just to be clear, you really didn't know?"

"I had no clue," she whispered.

"There was nothing normal about her life in L.A.," he said, handing her more pages.

This time, it was a series of screen captures. Images from Reagan's YouTube channel.

Diana leaned closer. At first glance, it was Reagan, surrounded by kids she often acted with and a few adults. It seemed harmless.

Then she realized she didn't recognize the video at all.

She'd never seen this footage before.

"What is this?" she asked.

"We gained access to her admin account," Sam said. "This was an unpublished video. Do you recognize anyone in these stills?"

"Just the kids from her videos. I'm assuming these are the parents?"

"No, these are sponsors."

"Sponsors?" For like the ads she would do? Diana wondered where he was going with this.

"Not exactly. These are the sponsors for the private events the kids would do."

"Private events?" Diana was feeling real fear.

He handed her the last piece of paper from the folder. It was a suggestive image of Reagan in a compromising position with one man from the first picture.

Diana dropped it like it burned her. Knowing what it meant. She stood, fists clenched, and lunged toward Sam. He scrambled off the stool, backing away fast. His brick wall persona cracked, and genuine surprise flickered across his face. The others stood frozen, like deer in headlights.

Her whole body rebelled against what her eyes and heart now knew to be true. And processing that on camera, surrounded by strangers, was more than she could bear.

This was the reaction he'd wanted. No warning. No mercy. Her pain was his payday.

"You motherfucker," she growled, voice breaking. "Get out of my house. I'm calling the cops."

"They know about this. They found it. I have an anonymous source who works for the police that sent me this, because they couldn't prioritize it."

"I don't give a fuck! Get out. This interview is over! You didn't come here to help. You came to feed on what's left of her."

Diana's hand went for her phone, and she started dialing her friend Detective Ray.

"Listen, Diana, I know this is a shock, but please believe me, we want to help. Do you trust me?" His eyes had softened. The brick wall was coming down layer by layer.

Every fear she and her mom had about Reagan growing up in that lifestyle was valid. And they hadn't done enough to protect her.

She should've seen it. Should've done something. And now here he was, trying to smooth it over, like his calm tone and practiced empathy made everything better. And the others were still just standing there. Hell, DeMarcus was probably still filming her.

But they were just the same as Layla. Exploiting Reagan.

Diana gripped her rage like a lifeline. Her fingers itched toward her waistband, toward her gun. Ordering them out at gunpoint would feel good. Justified... Almost.

But she forced a breath through clenched teeth, remembering her training: You can only point a gun at someone in the event of a deadly threat. This wasn't that.

"No, I don't trust you," she snapped. "I just fucking met you, and you've got the balls to show me this, with no warning? You wanted a podcast reaction? Well, buddy, you got one. Now leave!" She yelled, pointing towards the door.

"I know, I know, this is brand new evidence, and it changes everything. Let's take a break, and then let me tell you how I think we can help find her."

Diana was breathing hard, hand still on her phone, dialing Ray, but also itching just to drive them out of her house. The inner voice of guilt, said, you should have done more, made her nod her head.

She walked past Sam and Brent, not trusting herself to say another word, to head for the half bath under the stairs. Just a moment. She told herself. Just enough privacy to fix her face.

She stared at herself in the mirror. Tears leaked down her cheeks. She wiped them away with quick, angry swipes.

There was a powerful urge to punch the mirror. Or the wall. Or hell, maybe even Sam.

But none of that would fix this. None of that would help Reagan.

She hadn't done enough. That picture he showed her also proved she never had.

Another tear escaped. Then another. Her chest hitched, the sob rising hard in her throat, the threat of full-blown hysterics right behind it.

But she swallowed it down. Hard. She couldn't let it out. Not yet. Because as she stared into her own green eyes, she knew she deserved this pain. And it was nothing compared to what Reagan had survived.

A few minutes passed. Then a soft knock.

"Are you okay in there?" Sam asked. His voice was low and gentle.

Diana wiped away her tears and took a deep breath before she opened the door.

"I'm fine," she said. Although it was clear she wasn't. "Let's get this over with."

His eyes searched her face, and maybe there was another moment of empathy. He seemed to be aware that this interview had been a lot more painful than either of them could have expected.

But it was quickly quashed by his ambition to get the content for his podcast, as he warily followed her back to the sofa for the show to continue.

She kept her head down, not looking at any of them as they returned to their positions.

Sam resumed the questioning

"So that last picture was pretty disturbing,"

"To say the least," Diana replied. She made it very obvious she did not want to say anything more than absolutely necessary to finish this.

"How old do you think she was in that photo?"

"Why does that matter?"

"One of the biggest questions we have about this photo is if it was taken before or after she went missing." He explained. His tone was a lot softer than before.

Diana forced herself to look at the picture again. It was just shy of illicit material, but it was still very obvious what was going on. She needed to be looking for clues.

"She has bangs, and I can tell she has a zebra stripe manicure. No reason to think she couldn't have had both after she went missing and was older."

"But...." He led her to keep going.

"She also had gotten that haircut and that manicure the summer before she went missing, when she was only 14. But I know she had let her hair grow out by the time it was her birthday in September."

He said nothing, but nodded. Diana wrapped her arms around herself and was making a slow rocking motion. Trying to keep it together to finish this interview.

"What else do you know about her disappearance?" He asked. The warm intonation of his voice encouraged her to keep going.

"She was last seen by her co-star Bailey Jessica, where they filmed themselves walking along the Santa Monica Pier. She seemed in good spirits and said nothing about running away. Layla claims she woke up the next morning with her car gone, accounts drained, and a note saying goodbye forever."

"That sounds like a suicide note. Why would the police treat it like a runaway?" He was pushing her to get to the same conclusion he clearly had before he'd walked in here.

"That's a great question, possibly because of the money taken." She hypothesized.

"She could have done that just to hurt her mom? Doesn't mean she's a runaway. What did the police think?"

"They believed Layla. They notified harbor patrol, but no yachts had gone missing. And with the amount of cash Reagan took, she could have bought her own."

Diana took a moment to look back over everything she thought she knew and the additional evidence Sam had presented her with. Her thoughts swirling through pain, emotion, and curiosity.

"No, that's all wrong. They're looking in the wrong places." She said, finally looking up.

"I agree, and that's why I want to invite you to L.A. to look where they didn't." He said, surprising the shit out of her.

Diana was pretty sure her mouth was hanging open.

"What?"

"This case never got the right attention it needed. And although I could investigate alone, as I usually do. This would be the chance of a lifetime to have you there as Reagan's last living family member."

Diana just stared at him.

After a long moment of silence, she said.
"When do we leave?"

Chapter 3

Sam left Diana's house, heading to his rental car, still chewing on everything she'd said. Brent and DeMarcus had their own rental and were heading back to the hotel. But Sam decided he needed a drink.

After the bar fight in Nome, Alaska, he was infamous for, he'd avoided bars. But tonight, he felt off-kilter in a way he hadn't expected. His instincts were screaming, but his logical brain hadn't caught up yet. Maybe a drink and a little space to think would help.

The interview hadn't gone as expected. The details you could overlook, but then find out were actually important, was why it was so important to sit down and talk to people.

It hadn't registered with him before how young Diana had been when Reagan was born. And how she talked about Reagan with affection. Indicated they were a lot closer than he'd assumed. Or that Layla's checkered past was actually a non-factor.

He expected that angle because Reagan's YouTube channel hadn't featured them. And there had never been any social media posting of her visits to South Carolina.

Sam now understood that it had all been an attempt to protect her, and that Diana was torn between searching for Reagan and caring for her mother. It all made sense now.

Hell, he had realized she'd probably been waiting for a chance to do more and was grateful he was here to provide her with that opportunity.

It was actually refreshing to be so wrong about an assumption going into a story. That Jacob's family hadn't abandoned Reagan or held any type of

25

animosity against her.

He wasn't alone in his assumption. Brent had also figured she wouldn't want to talk to them, so they had planned to do a jump interview and approach her in public. But she'd accepted willingly. They expected her to be defensive, and to a degree, she was, but it was reasonable given the situation.

He'd really been shocked at the picture of them at the beach. The grand-mother in a beach chair, Reagan jumping in the air at the sandcastle they'd built, and Diana holding the camera in selfie style to capture it all.

Maybe he was getting too cynical in his old age. He was pushing 40, but life had taught him people are rarely what they seem, and this had been the first time that had been a good thing.

Brent had been the one to suggest right before they got here that they should invite Diana to L.A.. After seeing a picture of Diana, Sam knew why Brent was doing this. He was hoping to catch some sort of sparks flying after picking on him about his single status, knowing he had a thing for redheads.

Redheads with feisty personalities, just like Diana, as a matter of fact. This could be dangerous waters he was treading into. The way she went from gracious host offering them water, to a tearful aunt realizing the truth about her niece, to a Valkyrie ready to do battle with three grown men. Had him more smitten than he'd been in a long time.

Brent had probably meant it as a joke, but rather than think about how attractive he found her, he focused on that feeling of being pleasantly surprised after realizing how wrong he'd been about Diana. She seemed to be a good person. And that had been the deciding factor for him to take that risk and ask her to join them.

Part of the draw to this case had been showing how a child so famous could have had no one to turn to or advocate for her. He expected it to be similar to stories like Drew Barrymore or Britney Spears. Yet Reagan seemed to have that, if she had only asked. So now the question became, why did she never ask?

He was surprised he had to remind himself that he was there for an investigation about Reagan, when his instincts were more curious about Diana. He ignored that feeling and googled bars near him.

There had been an initial media frenzy when Reagan first went missing, but it died out quickly, as the public moved on. They chalked it up to poor little rich girl problems.

He was once again struck at how things for this case kept lining up. To the point it was begging him to investigate it. From the timing of the 5th anniversary, to evidence arriving in a timely fashion.

Also, the feeling that he needed a nice mainstream attention-grabbing case like this one to help him grow his podcast's reach after the first case proved it had substance.

There was a list of people to interview with Diana. The co-stars, the police investigators, and Layla's boyfriend, if they could find him.

Once they arrive in L.A., they would show Diana more of the evidence of what they'd found that they were hesitant to show in this initial interview.

He felt like he needed to establish some trust first and hadn't wanted to overwhelm her. And Brent had convinced him it would be better pacing for the show.

Now that he had a better sense of who she was and how committed she was to doing this, he regretted that choice. But he reminded himself, catching her reaction would be good for the show.

This was probably the reason he gravitated towards this case more than any of the other options that had a similar draw.

He really empathized with Reagan. Living a life in the spotlight was hard. As an adult, it was tricky. As a child, it would have been impossible.

As a content creator, he was always a little mindful of avoiding scandal. He didn't always succeed, but he had adapted and also learned how to use scandals to grow his viewership.

The messier the truth was he uncovered, both personally and professionally, the more the audience ate it up.

But after the cameras stopped rolling, there were also real consequences to deal with.

He headed to the nearest bar according to Google Maps and pulled into the Beachwood's Parking lot. It had been a bar, but was now a burnt pile of wood. He parked and looked at his phone again to find another option, but the sound of a car door had him looking around.

It was Diana.

He got out of the car to approach her. Wary about why she was also there.

"Did you follow me here?" He asked.

"No, I'm working." She pointed to the burned shell of a building behind him, its charred remains stark against the soft dunes and glint of water beyond.

"Ah...Arson?"

"Looks possible." She said, taking pictures of it. And the insurance building across the street. That puzzled him.

She clearly knew what she was doing, starting with wide-out pictures before moving closer to focus on details. It reminded him of the seasoned CSIs he'd met over the years.

The rash decision to invite her to LA was looking smarter and smarter by the second. Something he could definitely justify as necessary for her investigative skills and not more of because if they'd met in a bar, he would have approached her and asked for her number.

"So, this is what your day-to-day looks like?" He couldn't help but be curious. It was a professional hazard.

"Sometimes. When my mom was alive, I did a lot of the mundane stuff that kept me close to home. But my original passion for this job was because of the field work."

"And this field work couldn't wait?" He asked.

"If I'm leaving next week to meet you in L.A., I need to tie this up. Just out of curiosity, what are you doing here?" She asked.

"Looking for a drink, of course."

She gave him a small smile.

He was impressed. After everything they had just been through with the interview. Here she was, half an hour later, tying up loose ends so she could focus on Reagan's case.

Yet, feeling guilty about not telling her everything was really gnawing at him.

If there was a way to give her a heads up, that would preserve her reaction to the camera, now would be the time to say something... but then an unmarked police car also entered the parking lot, and a tall athletic guy in his mid-40's got out.

She gave that guy a big smile and a hug.

Sam's eyes narrowed, wondering what kind of relationship was presenting itself here. Was this her boyfriend? He had a wedding band on; was she sleeping with a married man? Or was he becoming too jaded and seeing lies, deceit, and secrets everywhere?

"This is Detective Ray Jordan. He's investigating this case. I asked him to meet me here so I can show him what I found."

"Do you work with him often?"

"Yeah, you'd be surprised how much local work there is here on the Grand Strand. Ray, this is the guy I told you about who was interviewing me about Reagan."

They shook hands, and Sam noticed there was a hard glint in Ray's eyes.

"So you're taking her to L.A. to investigate the disappearance?"

"Yeah, that's the plan."

"And what guarantees are you giving her that she'll be kept safe while she's out there?"

Sam looked at him, confused. He glanced at Diana, but she'd gone back towards the rubble to take more pictures and was out of earshot.

"L.A. is a dangerous place. She won't be able to bring her guns or conceal carry there because of their laws. And you're possibly opening a giant can of worms that isn't gonna want to be opened. I've seen your show. Things can turn dangerous for you as you confront people. Did you warn her about that?"

"Not really. We take every precaution."

Ray snorted. Sam got the feeling he knew about that incident in Nome, where things had gotten out of control.

"Precaution, my ass, you're what, 6'3, 225 lbs, and a former linebacker from Boston University. Look at her, she's maybe 5'6, 5'7, 150 lbs, she's more of a target than you are, asshole."

"Hey man, I'm not gonna let anything happen to her," Sam said defensively. He knew better than most that women lived in a different reality when it came to safety. God knows he'd covered enough of their stories over the years.

"You'd better. She's like a little sister to me and my wife's best friend, and if any harm comes to her, you can bet your pansy ass I will do the same to you."

"Message received." He told the detective. He didn't doubt the detective either, having met several guys like that when he did a tour with the Marines as an embedded journalist for a year. But he had no way of reassuring the guy that letting Diana get anywhere near danger was the last thing he wanted.

He may be well-known for his reckless streak when alone, but not when others were involved. That was one reason he hired a team to go with him after Nome.

Diana came back over to where they were standing in the parking lot.

"If you were looking for a drink, your best bet is up in Myrtle Beach. We were going to the Hanser House for dinner with his wife Traci, and they have a good cocktail menu if you'd like to join."

"I think I'll pass. I'll catch up with you at the airport on Sunday." He said after a moment. Spending too much time with her would make it harder to keep things professional. He could already tell that might be a problem.

As he headed north, his phone rang. It was DeMarcus.

"Hey man... where are you?" He asked.

"Heading to Myrtle Beach, why what's up?"

"I need you to stop and get a charger for my battery pack. I'm hoping they have one at Walmart. Brent accidentally stepped on mine and broke the prong out."

"Really? Ok... and neither of you has a spare?" He was pretty sure DeMarcus had brought an entire bag of just cords for stuff.

"He didn't say he had one. He said sorry and that he needed some space and went for a walk."

"Yeah, I can imagine with him being a dad that this case may hit a little close to home for him," Sam said.

God knows it was grim stuff.

"I suppose...but if you can just get a spare while you're out, that would be great."

"Sure, text me exactly what you need, and I'll see what they've got. It never hurts to have a spare."

"Thanks, man. I'll tell Brent to be a little less clumsy next time."

"Be nice...we don't need a bunch of drama with Diana joining us in L.A.."

"Whatever you say, man...but.... Drama seems to follow you."

Sam hung up on him.

He was smiling, though. DeMarcus was right. Drama seemed to follow him.

But maybe because that's where the stories were.

Chapter 4

As Diana got into the car to leave the Hanser House restaurant, she hesitated.

Today had been a lot. Getting to hang out with Ray and Traci had been great, but they were getting to go home together to their kids.

Diana didn't have anyone waiting for her at home. The loneliness she'd been feeling since her mom died was back with a vengeance tonight.

"Fuck it, I need a drink." She muttered to herself and headed north.

Maybe she would get into a bar fight and take out the rage she felt on someone who underestimated her, or let a hot guy pick her up.

She snorted with laughter at that thought. She talked a good game, but never had casual sex. Ever. But the feeling of wanting to do something reckless was driving her.

She found a parking spot near the beachfront bar where her car would be safe overnight, because she was going to Uber home. Before she got out, she locked her gun in the car safe. Since drinking was going to be on the agenda today, the gun had to stay here.

She grabbed her tactical hair sticks just so she had at least one defensive option, just in case.

It was still early compared to normal party hours, so she could get a seat at the bar pretty quickly.

"I'm gonna need a Long Island Iced Tea, and three shots of Jack, please." She told the bartender.

They quickly got her drinks poured and set them out in a row in front of her.

Diana stared at them. The responsible adult side of her made her hesitate.

She had to decide whether she was committed to being as reckless as her heart was begging for, or not.

The pain and emotion that were barely being held back threatened to spill over at any moment, and she knew she would soon be spiraling. And god help her, if she started spiraling, she was going to do so with a drink in her hand.

Diana did each of the shots, one right after the other, in single gulps. The fire of the whiskey burned her throat. Then she chugged the full glass of Long Island Iced Tea.

As she set the glass down, she noticed the bar had gotten kind of quiet, and she noticed several pairs of eyes on her from around the room.

"Thank you, I just need one more Jack and Coke and that'll close out my tab for the night." She said, handing the bartender her credit card.

She could nurse this drink for an hour and then be ready to go home.

She moved to a seat in the corner of the bar and pulled out her phone to go through all the old pictures of Reagan.

Being in the bar's corner gave her a little feeling of privacy, even as the crowd swelled with a bunch of college kids there for spring break.

She hoped most of the people in the room could read her body language as fuck off. Because she knew if someone tried to pull her into conversation, there was about a 50/50 chance she'd either break a beer bottle over their head or kiss them. Neither for any good reason, except that the reckless feeling had taken over.

From a young age, she'd been the responsible one. "The Good Kid." Her dad had gotten cancer when she was 13 and refused chemo. And Jacob was always a bit of a wild child. So Diana tried to stay out of trouble to not add any stress to her mother.

Even in college, when all the other kids were drinking and partying and making bad decisions. She was usually the designated driver, the one making sure everyone got home ok while still making the honor roll.

She never had space to be dumb, reckless, or irresponsible, and for one night, she wanted to hang up her protector shield and dive deep into just feeling. To embrace the chaos instead of trying to bend it to her will.

****

Sam was surprised when he saw Diana walk into the same bar he'd found.

He was shocked to see her down several drinks and then slink off to the corner to scroll on her phone.

Was she meeting someone here? Did she have a boyfriend? She had nothing like that on her social media. And he tried hard not to think about why her relationship status was so important to him. But as Sam watched her, he noticed. Silent tears were streaming down her face, and he knew.

This was about today. Guilt washed over him as he watched her for a while, realizing she didn't have much of a support system to help her through this.

His booth was on the opposite side of the bar from hers. For the moment, they were both being left alone by the crowd. But it wouldn't last. He knew it was inevitable someone else would see her.

An older guy, maybe in his 40s, who looked like an aging cast member of Jersey Shore, approached her. He was clearly there to ogle girls. Then he leaned over Diana, caging her in the corner.

Sam didn't hesitate; he got up and started heading her way.

He couldn't hear what they were talking about or see her expression. But one thing he could see was the guy slipping something into her drink while she wasn't looking.

"Fuck." He said under his breath, then a girl bumped into him and her drink spilled. A college kid with her took offense to that. Just as he ducked, he pushed the guy next to Sam.

Keep moving. He thought. However, he could hear the chaos of a fight start behind him.

He watched her take a sip of her drink.

"Shit! Fuck! He mumbled, pushing more people out of his way.

The bar was so packed, and with the fight growing behind him, people weren't watching where they were going and blocking the walkable area he needed to get to her.

He was about 10 yards away when he could tell whatever was happening to her was happening now. The guy dragged her off her bar stool and was heading towards a back exit.

Sam was right on their heels as the exit door closed behind them.

He caught up before they hit the pavement from the sidewalk that wrapped around the building.

"Hey man, where are you taking her?" He said, pulling on the guy's shoulder to make him turn around.

"Ahh, yeah, this is my girlfriend. She wanted to go home. It was getting kind of rowdy in there."

"Girlfriend, really? What's her name?"

"Sarah..."

Sam didn't wait for him to finish his sentence before cold cocking him in the face.

The guy's nose made a very satisfying crushing noise, and he fell to the ground. Diana looked surprised.

Part of him wanted to continue to beat the shit out of him, but his concern was for Diana, and getting her away from danger was far more pressing.

Also, reasonable force dictated that now that the threat was over, he should stop. Or the police might think he was the attacker.

"Diana, that guy put something in your drink, are you ok?" He asked, peering into her green eyes to see if they were constricting or dilating. Hell, how could he tell what either of those symptoms meant?

"I'm...a little woozy..." she slurred. Not sure if it was the alcohol or whatever this guy did, but the guy was trying to get up again.

"She told me her name was Sarah..." the guy said.

"Yep, because girls never need to lie to creeps like you," Sam said. Anger was pouring from him. What if he hadn't been here? A woman alone like her shouldn't have been this reckless.

"I'm...gonna...kick your ass..." Diana slurred and then attempted to kick the man, but wobbled horribly off balance. Her shoe went flying off her foot.

Sam caught her, pulling her to his chest.

"That's a lot...harder ...when you.. drink..."

"I'm calling the cops.." Sam said, moving her so he could get to his phone.

The man made a run for it, and Sam noted the car he jumped into. A black

BMW. It headed northbound on the boulevard.

Sam was already on the phone with 911 and told them everything. But squad cars arrived before he'd even disconnected. Presumably to deal with the bar fight inside.

"Ok, I'm gonna deal with them and then I'll take you home. But right now, I want you to wait in my car." He swept her up into his arms to carry her to his rental.

She gave a small yelp and looked surprised. But then she leaned into his embrace as he carried her.

"Sam...the hunter...the truth hunter. That's what you should have named your show." She said, reaching up to pat the side of his face with a mischievous smile on her lips.

It wasn't a half-bad name, he thought, depositing her into his passenger seat. He went back inside to pay his tab and make sure he had her purse before returning to his car.

He waved an officer over, who came and got their information. He kept his statement brief as he grabbed the shoe that had gone flying.

"About the time the fight started, I saw a guy slip something into her drink and try to leave with her. I know her, so I followed, but I stopped him, and he ran off."

The officer nodded, writing what he'd said. Sam turned back to Diana, sitting in his passenger seat.

"You know I should probably take you to the ER to get checked out, no telling what he put in your drink," Sam said as the officer radioed in the description and direction of travel for a BOLO to dispatch.

"No.. home. I'm fine. Just tired."

Sam could see the sadness wash over her face as it crumbled. Tears started leaking out of the sides of her eyes, before she covered her face with her hands.

He didn't really know this woman, and yet, after days of doing research on her and her family, he felt a lot of empathy for her in this moment. The guilt of dropping all of this on her was making him feel responsible for her safety.

Hell, he should be thanking her. After having to show her that picture of Reagan tonight, and knowing what likely has happened to her. It felt good to punch someone. Part of him wondered if that hadn't been her plan when she didn't resist being pulled out of the bar.

"I still think I should get you checked out." He said, touching her face to have her look at him, so he could assess if the drugs were affecting her.

"I never... swallowed." She said, still slurring her words, but not too badly.

"Wait, a second.. what's going on here?" He asked. The cop also looked surprised.

She took a moment to wipe her eyes.

"I clocked him before he ever got to me and knew he would try something. My plan was to get to my car, where my gun was, and hold him at gunpoint till the cops arrived, but you 'rescued' me first."

"What the hell? Diana!" Sam was shocked. The cop laughed.

"If you're alright, ma'am, you're free to go," He said before heading back inside.

"Thank you, Officer Hennigan." She called out.

Sam got into the driver's seat.

"It's fine. After today, I just felt like I needed to go out. Maybe to punch someone, fuck someone, or do something out of the norm for me. Vigilante seemed like a good compromise. Sadly, my night was spoiled."

She was crazy; that was the only explanation. Well, that's what he should have thought. Yet, what she said mirrored how he'd felt when he remembered how much he'd enjoyed punching that guy in the face.

"Do you do that often? Vigilante shit?" He asked, starting the car and turning south.

"God no. I am a very boring person. I get up, I work, I watch TV, play video games, or read books. I go to bed, and I do it all again the next day. Actually, it was pretty stupid of me. Rule number one of self-defense: never put yourself in a situation where you need it."

"No shit. It was risky as hell." Was he lecturing a woman he barely knew? Yes. Did it still need to be said... also yes. He was angry with her. What if he hadn't been there?

Diana kept talking. Completely ignoring him.

"But tonight I needed a drink, and I knew there was a chance someone would bother me, so I had this as a backup plan." She said, gesturing to the hairsticks he noticed hadn't been there when he saw her before. "But honestly, this is probably better. If my plan had worked, the cops would have wanted a statement, but I can imagine if I asked a lawyer, they would tell me to wait till I was sober."

"No kidding. Do you usually drink this much when you go out?"

"No, I haven't drunk this much since college. Never liked the taste of beer or wine, so when we'd play drinking games. I always had Jack, or Captain, with me."

"Jesus, you're gonna feel that tomorrow, Diana."

"Nope, I'll wake up at 9 am and be hungry." She sounded very sure of herself.

"We'll see about that." He said grimly.

He continued to drive to her house. A sense of being in shock and a tiny bit of awe at who Diana seemed to be. Feisty, to say the least.

He pulled into her driveway and went around to open the car door for her. She'd fallen asleep.

"Hey, Diana, we're here."

A sleepy eye opened up at him, and she smiled.

His heart did a somersault. She looked so beautiful when she was waking up.

She leaned up and kissed his cheek.

"Thank you for driving me home." She said with a yawn.

She got out of his rental and walked up to her front door. He lingered behind her a few steps and noticed she hesitated.

"Is something wrong?" Sam asked after a few moments of her not moving.

"It's just me being silly..."

"I doubt that."

"I'm throwing a little pity party for myself because after a hard day where I found out I am a total failure as an aunt, and let a potential date rape guy get away, that there's no one inside waiting for me to give me a hug and tell me it's all gonna be ok. And it's making me a little sad."

"That's not silly. And you're not a total failure, and I'm sure they'll catch that guy."

He hesitated a moment, but walked up to her and said,

"But if you need a hug, come here." He said before pulling her into his arms.

She came willingly, and Sam wrapped his arms around her, gently stroking the back of her head.

"It's all going to be okay," he murmured, even if he wasn't sure it was true.

The scent of jasmine rose from her hair. Probably her shampoo. He thought.

A wave of longing crept in, uninvited. If only they'd met under different circumstances. He could lean into this moment, savor it even. But right now, he had to cling to his professionalism with both hands.

Because God, it had been such a long time since someone needed him like this. And the line was starting to blur between him just trying to be a decent guy and something that was starting to feel personal. That's the thought to cling to: You're just being a gentleman. Sam thought, pulling himself out of the moment.

Doing what any other decent man would do after a day like this, hell, after the day they both had. Showing up to an interview, not knowing what to expect. Gambling your second season on a story that could make or break your career. Watching a woman, clearly strong, clearly hurting, receive devastating news and still choose to fight.

It hadn't been easy for him either. Asking the questions that needed to be asked. Pushing her past the outrage when she wanted to throw him out. Keeping evidence from her.

Always putting the podcast first was wearing on him. He thought with a sigh. But he could not deny that he probably needed this hug as much as she did.

After a few moments, she pulled away slightly and said, "Thank you. You're a lot kinder than I thought you would be. I expected to get railroaded by you, and not in a good way, either. You know, in the interview. But you didn't emotionally beat me up too much. Thank you for that."

He couldn't help but laugh at her joke.

"I just want the truth. No emotional beat down needed, because other than trying to trap criminals, I don't think you have a false bone in your body."

She gave him a wicked smile and mumbled something under her breath as she unlocked the front door. He could have sworn she said something about a different type of bone in her body, but he chose to ignore that.

"Did you want to come inside? I'd hate to make you drive all the way back to your hotel this late."

He could read between the lines and knew she was offering a one thing that could lead to another type of invitation. As much as he wanted to agree, he hesitated. She'd been drinking and was emotionally wrecked today, by him nonetheless. The smart thing would be to say goodnight now and leave.

But he was surprised at how much he wanted to take her up on that offer. He knew exactly what to say and exactly what to do, and he could spend the night in her bed, rather than the cold, lonely hotel up the street.

Almost involuntarily, his hand reached up to tuck a stray hair behind her ear.

"It's alright, I'll be back in the morning and we'll go get your car. You just need to get some sleep. Then we can test that theory on whether you wake up with the worst hangover in the world or not."

She laughed.

"Ok fine, for losing this bet. Bring me a chicken biscuit in the morning because I'm gonna be hungry."

"And what happens if I win?" He asked with a grin.

"You won't, but if you just want something on the table. I'll cook you breakfast if you win."

"Deal." He said, and they shook hands. He couldn't help but notice how beautiful she looked in the moonlight. He watched her close the door and heard her lock it.

As he returned to his car, he felt something he couldn't put a name to. He was eager to see her again, and he couldn't remember the last time he felt this way, because he knew this feeling had nothing to do with his podcast.

****

The next morning, her phone rang at 9 a.m. It was Sam.

Diana winced. This was going to be awkward. She'd invited him to stay, and he'd turned her down. What the hell had she been thinking? She knew exactly what she'd been thinking.

Walking into an empty house after a day like that had been too much to bear. Drinking more than she should, making reckless choices... it had felt easier than sitting alone with the loneliness and guilt.

"And how's the hangover?" Sam asked, his voice tinged with humor.

"What hangover?" she replied with a yawn, pushing herself upright in bed.

Her mouth was dry, her stomach was growling, and the sunlight stabbing through the blinds made her squint, but nothing she'd call a real hangover.

"What, nothing?" He said, clearly astonished.

"I told you, I don't get hangovers. My liver is built like a tank," she replied with a smile.

"Fine, I'll get you a chicken biscuit. Meet me outside, and I'll take you to get your car."

"I was kidding, Sam. You don't have to do this."

"Well, it's also convenient. I'm having DeMarcus tag along. We thought it would be a good idea to do a tour of the area and see the places you would take Reagan when she was here. Our flight leaves tomorrow morning, so today is the only day we have to do this."

"Ok, I'll be down there in about 15 minutes. I just woke up." She told him while getting out of bed and heading towards the bathroom.

"Wait, you're a rare woman if you can get ready that fast." He sounded genuinely surprised.

"Sweetheart. I could be ready in 5, but I figured you'd appreciate me taking a shower first."

He chuckled. "My mistake, take all the time you need. We're not in a rush today."

"Nope, now you've made it a challenge. I'll see you in 10," she said, turning on the shower and hanging up.

She walked out to her driveway with moments to spare, with her challenge. Knowing she would be on camera, she wore a ball cap and sunglasses with her hoodie and leggings. Opting to be more comfortable than classy.

Something about wearing the hat and glasses made her feel like she had body armor on. She'd let her guard down with Sam last night and felt exposed.

Today, her defenses were back in place, right where they belonged.

Any personal detail Sam picked up could be used against her later in the edit bay. Every slip of emotion? Potential podcast gold. And she wasn't about to hand him more material than she already had. The fact that she found him attractive was painfully obvious.

That cat was already out of the bag. The others? They needed to stay in their damn crates.

"You look great," Sam said, holding the passenger door open.

DeMarcus was posted up in the back seat, camera on his lap, giving her a nod and a friendly smile.

Diana slid into the seat and buckled in. She kept her mouth shut, barely. Every part of her wanted to volley something flirty back. Because damn if he didn't look good too.

Yesterday, he'd been all buttoned up authority, sport coat, polished tone, firm questions.

But this morning he was wearing a T-shirt, gym shorts, and flip-flops.

This version of Sam was more laid back and approachable. It was dangerous as hell.

Because she couldn't help but pray this man never buys another razor, as his five o'clock shadow was close to making her forget everything else that was going on.

Diana gave them a tour around town, showing them the different places they would frequent when Reagan came to visit. It had always been such a special time. They tried to pack as much fun and normal kid stuff into her visits as possible.

"Here is the water park we would take her to." She said, pointing at what used to be Wild Water and Wheels.

"And here we rode go-karts." She said as they passed the Broadway Grand Prix.

"Family Kingdom is down that way; we'd make a trip there every year, too."

"What was the favorite trip you remember?" Sam asked.

A warm smile spread across Diana's face.

"When she begged to go to Ripley's Haunted Adventure. I was supposed to be following her with my hand on her shoulder, but an actor snuck in front of me, and she didn't realize it for a good two to three minutes until we got into an elevator. The look on her face was...priceless."

Sam smiled at the story. Almost too quickly, they arrived at the bar, and she was picking up her car.

DeMarcus waited in the rental as he was dealing with a battery issue with his camera, so she and Sam had a moment alone outside of the car.

"Oh, I forgot to tell you," she said. "I texted Ray last night about what happened. He texted me back. They caught that guy. Got it all on the bar's security cams. He's going to jail. He was hoping to have us come in this afternoon to give official statements."

She hesitated. "I don't remember if you fully explained what happened, but I know they're gonna ask about his face. I was thinking I'd just say he fell..."

"No. Don't do that." His voice was quiet. Firm. It stopped her cold.

"Do what?" she asked, confused.

"Lie for me."

He stepped closer. His eyes locked on hers.

"I punched him in the face. And I'd do it again. I accept whatever consequences come with that." He said, not breaking his piercing blue gaze from her eyes.

The air between them shifted. The way the moment sizzled had her heart slamming against her ribs.

Then he blinked. He stepped back, casual again.

Diana tried to pull herself together. But couldn't help but think if this had been another time. He would have made a great Warrior Knight.

"Considering I thought he was kidnapping you," he added lightly, "I doubt there'll be any trouble. Send me your friend's number. I'll write the statement."

She handed over the phone, fingers slightly numb.

She didn't say a word.

But internally? That was hot. Unapologeticly accountable was so fucking hot.

Chapter 5

Diana had traveling down to a science. One checked bag with 90% of her things, one backpack for her carry-on, and her wallet consolidated to a cross-body phone strap for ease of use at the airport.

She found Sam and his crew at the terminal waiting. It looked like they also liked to get there early.

"Hi," she said in greeting.

"You made it," Sam said from where he was sitting. A tablet was open on his lap, and he had earbuds in.

"Yep, thanks for the ticket." She said, sitting next to Sam.

"So I've been thinking. If Reagan never talked to me, or as far as I know, my mom, about what was going on out there. Is it possible she talked to her friends about it?"

"We shall see. We came to you first, so we are really starting from the beginning on looking into things." He said.

"Did you have a list of the friends you want to talk to?" She asked.

"Her co-stars, yes," Sam said, taking his earbuds out in an obviously annoyed way. It pissed her off.

"No. Not her co-stars, her friends. She had friends outside of the business she would talk about. From school."

"Do you remember their names?" He asked with raised eyebrows. Brent, it seemed, thought it was worth writing down as he took out a notebook.

"Not really, but I bet her teachers would know." Everyone looked disappointed.

"Brent, add them to the list." He said, not looking at her. Going back to what was clearly something important on his tablet.

"Great, I just wanted to mention it while I was thinking about it. You can go back to whatever it was you were doing."

It came out a little ruder than she intended, but he said nothing and put his earbuds back in, and she pulled out her book to read.

"What is that?" Brent asked.

"A book that was recommended on booktok."

"Yeah, I recognize it. What do you think so far?"

"It's a little weird. The premise is serial killers who fall in love, and yet I can't help but keep reading. This is the third book in the series."

"My ex-wife loved to read." He looked really sad all of a sudden.

"So you're divorced?"

"Yeah, it's kind of recent. Which is why getting a fresh start with Sam here has been such a blessing."

"So you just started working for him? What's it like?"

"Great, so far. This is my first case. I used to work in project management, so it's a natural fit. Getting all the pieces together, working, and making the show run smoothly. I love it."

"I bet."

"Well, I'll let you get back to your book. I've got editing work to do."

"It's a good distraction. I've been binge-watching all of Reagan's old videos, and I really needed a break."

Sam interjected.

"Any clues?"

"Not really. I started with the stuff from when she was little, and it's all so cringey now."

"Cringey, how?"

"One video was of her in a bubble bath. I remember my mom and I raising hell over that one. But Layla assured us she had on a bathing suit underneath, and you can barely make it out. She wasn't lying, but it still looks...weird."

"Like the kind of thing that would bring the child predators out of the woodwork?" Sam countered.

Diana nodded. "It did."

Diana glanced around and noticed DeMarcus was filming. This time with his phone. He was trying not to be obvious about it, but she could tell.

"Yeah, I majored in Criminal Justice. This was right after I graduated from college, and Layla said I was paranoid and feeding into my mom's paranoia. She threatened to stop the visits if we didn't 'Get a grip.' So my mom asked me to lay off Layla about it. And to my knowledge, she never did things like suggested nudity again."

"How old do you think she was in that video?" Sam asked.

"She would have been 8."

"Perhaps something else to tell the police when we arrive," Sam said.

Diana nodded.

They went back to waiting, and Diana tried to read, but her gaze kept getting distracted by Sam. So she tried to distract herself by watching Brent and DeMarcus. Brent reminded her of her mechanic. A no BS, get shit done type. Like a bulldozer. But he was a teddy bear once you got to know him.

DeMarcus was young and athletic, but seemed shy and mild-mannered, which was an interesting contrast to the Hunter and the Bulldozer types the others were.

Like he was born to be behind the camera. Quiet, calm, and steady. He was currently talking on the phone. Diana deduced it was his mom. They seemed close.

Just then, the gate agent came over the loudspeaker announcing that boarding was about to begin. This would be her first time in first class. Sam had been very generous with the tickets. And she'd gotten a window seat.

Flying always made her a little nervous, so being able to see what was going on helped. As she took her seat, she was a little surprised to notice Sam had the seat next to her.

He was still on his tablet with his earbuds in, and she could see now he was looking at metric data. Probably for his podcast to see how many viewers he had for last week's episode. This was the business side of running a podcast.

As the plane made its way to the runway, Diana gripped the armrest and carefully watched the landscape outside change and then fall away as the plane lifted into the air. It was going out over the ocean, and she jumped a little when the landing gear clicked into place underneath them.

A warm hand enveloped hers, and she looked at Sam.

"You good?" he asked.

"Yeah, it's just takeoffs and landings I get nervous about."

He released her hand. But she could still feel its warmth.

"So tell me about yourself, outside of being Reagan's aunt." He asked.

She couldn't help but look around to see if DeMarcus was somehow filming this, and he chuckled.

"Sorry, this is just me asking. Since we're going to be spending quite a lot of time together, I wanted to get to know you better."

"So you'll know which emotional heartstrings to tug at when the cameras are rolling?"

"I can see how you'd think that, and I can't say I haven't used personal knowledge in an interview before."

"I know. I saw the interview you did with your ex-wife. The one right after you quit the Post."

"Oh..."

"I mean, as someone who is typically in favor of the idea, an eye for an eye and being petty, it was fabulous. Telling her it was an interview about how working with your spouse at the same company can be tricky, and then railroading her with the evidence that she was sleeping with your best friend on a live interview. It was .... I'm not even sure what to call it, but it certainly got your podcast off to a great start. Then your work with the Missing and Murdered Indigenous women was inspiring, really."

He was silent and just stared at her.

"But I get it. You want to find the truth. The painful, hard-to-look-at sometimes, truth. Even if it takes manipulating people to get it."

"And is this your warning that you can't be manipulated?" He asked after he'd taken a moment to process what she had said.

Diana gave a small laugh.

"I'm human. Of course, I can be manipulated, the warning is, I'm also petty and believe in revenge. So just tread carefully."

He grinned at that.

"Duly noted."

After a few moments, he continued.

"So let's start somewhere safe. How did you become an insurance claims adjuster?"

"Well, like I mentioned, I went to school for Criminal Justice. I'd always wanted to go into law enforcement and be a detective. My Dad had been a cop in the military, so it felt natural to want to do that. He died before Jacob did. Thank God, that would have killed him. But due to a knee injury, trying to complete all the conditioning in the academy is basically impossible. So I thought this would be the next best thing."

"I'm sorry about your knee."

"Yeah, me too. I was doing martial arts and didn't move fast enough and shattered my patella."

"Jesus, I bet that hurt."

"0 out of 0 stars, would not recommend."

He chuckled.

"And what about outside of work? What do you like to do?"

She paused. When her mom had been alive, every spare moment outside of work revolved around taking care of her. When was the last time she'd done something fun just for herself?

"What are you trying to ask? Do you like long walks on the beach, Pina Coladas, and getting caught in the rain?"

He laughed again.

"Then the answer is no. I actually hate the beach, too much sand and too many tourists. I prefer Daiquiris over Pina Coladas as I'm allergic to coconut, and rain here usually comes with lightning, so I'll keep my ass in the house, actually."

"You're funny," he said.

"I mean, someone has to be. Y'all are all very serious types of people. And I know this is a serious case, but God, life is too short to be serious all the time."

"I agree." His smile was doing things to her, so she decided to tone it down.

Even though flirting with him was fun.

"But in all seriousness. I wasn't lying when I said I'm boring. I get up, go to work, I come home, I read books, watch TV, or sometimes play video games. Occasionally, I'll tag along with Ray and Traci to the gun range, or travel to the mountains where I went to college for football games because I like to see leaves that actually change color. But yeah. I'm boring."

He took that in, but before he could ask her another question. She asked one.

"What about you? Tell me about yourself."

He looked a little surprised at that.

"Nope, it's my turn to interview you. How did you get into being a Podcaster...other than the obvious, you were an investigative journalist."

He shifted in his seat slightly.

"Well, I guess it started when I was a kid. I really liked Superman comics, and since I couldn't be Superman, I became Clark Kent."

"Bullshit."

He looked surprised.

"I know about the car accident and how you had to clear your name from the drunk deputy who tried to pin it on you."

"How in the hell..."

"Insurance claims adjuster," Diana said, pointing at her head. Like that would explain how she knew that.

He just stared at her.

"You do realize uncovering the truth in that case to the point where people would believe you was probably a huge factor in your career, right? Why not bring it up?"

He looked away, as if trying to decide how much to tell.

"One thing you learn is that the truth is not always so cut and dry. Yes, the deputy was drinking earlier. Was he drunk? No. But I discovered he'd been meeting a woman at the bar, and he was married, and so was she. She wouldn't leave her husband for him because of her son. So he'd actually been trying to get rid of the husband and make it look like an accident, not realizing it was the son who was driving."

Diana's mouth fell open. He was the son.

"Wow."

She couldn't help but pat him on the arm. Realizing that finding out was not only traumatic because it had been a serious accident, but it also would have destroyed his parents' marriage and his trust in people for a long time.

And then his wife basically did the same thing by breaking his trust and cheating on him. No wonder he's so ruthless about the truth.

"Well, not to sound mean or anything, but at least you didn't shatter your patella."

It was a hearty laugh that erupted out of him.

"Yeah, my kneecaps are fine, just shattered my collarbone, ankle, and lower leg."

"But you must have recovered quickly because you played football in college?"

"Yeah, but it was also the first thing mentioned in every scouting report by the NFL."

"That's ok, although there's a lot of fame and fortune in professional football, I think we both know you're exactly where you are supposed to be. Still with fame and clearly fortune, with fewer concussions and booked weekends."

"You'd be surprised. I still work a lot of weekends."

"Considering it's Sunday and we're traveling for your job, I would say that's pretty obvious, but you're running this ship, not the NFL."

"Touche."

"So, your turn. Do you like long walks on the beach, and all that jazz?"

He laughed again.

"Sure, with the right company."

She looked at him, waiting for him to elaborate.

"But most of my free time is spent researching, networking, and hitting the gym to stay sane." He continued.

He was a big guy. Not just in size, but muscle too. She could tell from the way his button-down shirt fitted across his shoulders. He must not miss the gym often. Not to mention when he carried her to the car at the bar. Which, even in her drunken stupor, she had to admit, was impressive.

"See, that's where you and I differ. I hate the gym. I'd much rather do an activity than just working out for workout's sake. However, I do like doing martial arts. May as well learn something useful."

And actually... he was exactly the kind of sparring partner she would love to meet on the mat. If only they had met under those circumstances.

The flight attendant with the beverages came by, and after she left, Diana asked.

"So tell me about your guys. How did they end up working with you?"

"Brent came highly recommended by one of my sponsors, and DeMarcus's mom does my taxes and needed a job. He's actually very talented, so it works out, even though I used to do my own camerawork with a tripod."

"See, I knew you had a soft spot. That is so sweet, offering him a job."

He rolled his eyes, but the smile tugging at his lips said he was biting back something less appropriate. She didn't press, but she didn't miss it either.

This was fun. Breaking the tension and getting to know him on a more personal level really helped calm some of the anxiety she felt about this entire trip. Going to a place she'd never been before, with people she barely knew. It was a lot to be nervous about. Let alone knowing that at any moment she could find out what really happened to Reagan, and her reaction would be caught on camera for millions of people to watch. Good, bad, or otherwise.

Considering they would be in Atlanta soon for their layover, she decided she would enjoy this brief part of her journey. Delaying the reality of what they were getting themselves into with this investigation.

"So tell me, Sam, what's been your favorite part of being a podcaster?" She asked.

Moving the conversation back into safer, more professional waters. He was exactly her type: tall, broad-shouldered, smart, good sense of humor. Dark hair and blue eyes, man, if only he had a beard, he'd be perfect.

But with the hard lines of his face, it was easier to remember they were there for more serious business. The reality was that his podcast would always come first. And therein lay the danger of letting him know her too well because they were going to start an emotional roller coaster once they arrived in L.A.

Chapter 6

Sam had really enjoyed getting to know Diana more. It almost felt like a date, the way she was making him laugh. With a bit of teasing and flirting. But she would always bring it back to the business that brought them together. And Sam was once again feeling like it was a shame they hadn't met under different circumstances.

She'd fallen asleep on the longer flight from Atlanta, and her head had ended up on his shoulder. The soft rise and fall of her chest had captivated him like no other woman had in a very long time. And for a moment, he could forget everything to do with his show and just sit and enjoy her company. Her presence. And the way she was starting to make him feel.

That maybe there was hope that someone would see the man beneath the podcaster.

Brent and DeMarcus had the seats across the aisle from them on this flight, and they were both immature assholes enough to give him a sarcastic thumbs up and make kissy faces at them while she was sleeping. He had flipped them off.

He'd been in a bad mood due to hotel issues while they were at the airport. But she had quickly gotten him out of his grumpy mindset with her banter and positive attitude. She had shown off her investigative chops by researching him and not just reading the headlines, but understanding the story between the lines. He felt seen by her in a way that made him crave more.

Now they were in L.A. on the way to their Airbnb. He opted for that after the issue with the hotel. Which he wasn't even mad about because it meant more privacy for her. Since the investigation would be pulling at her emotional heartstrings. Privacy would be key in the coming days.

The conversation on the plane had given him a lot of insights into her personality.

She was smart, funny, and cut through bullshit like she had a knife. She had a real joie de vivre personality. Diana was also very self-aware and knew better than most what she was likely to find on this journey and bravely came anyway. It impressed the hell out of him.

He pulled the rented SUV to the house in a quiet neighborhood close to where Layla and Reagan lived.

"Do you need a hand with your bags?" He asked Diana as they jumped out of the car in the driveway.

"I got it. I've never stayed in an Airbnb before. How does this work?" She asked.

"I figured you'd take the master since it has an en-suite, and the rest of us will share the other bedrooms and bathrooms. Brent is gonna order some groceries so we have snacks and stuff on hand. Did you have any requests?"

"Peanut M&M's, Chocolate Pop-Tarts. Sour Cream and Onion Chips. I guess would be my comfort food, but typically I'm good with just a ham or tuna sandwich. If this place has a grill, you could splurge and get steaks. It could be nice."

"We'll take a look."

The house was beautiful, not a mansion, but just a nice-sized family home with a modern Spanish aesthetic.

He had picked this house, not only because it provided her some privacy with a downstairs master suite, while he and the guys had three bedrooms and two bathrooms upstairs. It also had a formal living room they could set up to do the interviews in, which was separate from the rest of the living area.

While Brent was getting groceries, DeMarcus was going to get some other supplies, including a giant whiteboard. So they could lay all the evidence out to analyze Reagan's last movements. It's not something they really needed, but it looked good for the cameras.

So he and Diana had the house to themselves for a while. There was a strong urge to seek her out to engage in more of the flirty banter from the plane.

However, the closer they got to LA, the quieter she'd gotten. And he noticed the less focus she could keep on him, or her book, or really anything except silently looking out the window.

He set his bag down in the upstairs bedroom that would be his. Since he was the one paying for everything, he got the other room with a private bath while Brent and DeMarcus had a Jack and Jill bath between their rooms.

He always liked to take a shower after flying all day, so he followed that routine before looking for Diana.

He found her in the backyard by the pool. She had changed into a bathing suit. It was a black one-piece with white accents around the bust and waist that was stunning on her. He couldn't help but let his gaze linger on her curves and long legs before opening the back door.

"I see you found the pool?" He said, stepping out onto the back porch.

"Yeah, I brought a bathing suit just in case, and figured before we get dinner or whatever, I would enjoy the backyard."

"I was hoping to go over tomorrow's agenda. Breakfast by 8, we'll roll some video in that living room, and basically just lay out our game plan of investigation. We plan to meet the detective around noon and then use the afternoon to track down people who knew Layla and Reagan. We'll hopefully wrap up a decent day one with dinner and then film some more after dinner to recap what we learned."

Diana nodded.

"It's a grueling pace, and if you need a break, please let me know. I don't want to ...what was the phrase you used, tug at your emotional heartstrings anymore than is absolutely necessary."

"I know it sounds harsh, but the more I can compartmentalize, the faster we can get answers. So that is my focus, and you don't have to worry about my emotional heartstrings."

Sam studied her. Stubbornness was etched into every line of her face. But beneath it, he recognized something deeper.

Desperation.

He knew that look. The kind of tunnel vision that comes when you're chasing answers because the silence is too loud to live with. Cases like this, ones with heartbreak around every corner, were dangerous. Especially when there was no guarantee they'd find anything at all.

And for someone like Diana? Someone who'd clearly spent years torn by the responsibility she felt towards her family, between her mom and Reagan? She wouldn't just be disappointed if the trail went cold. She'd be wrecked.

What scared him more was knowing she didn't seem to have anyone waiting in the wings to catch her if she fell. He swallowed hard. He hadn't meant to feel responsible for her. But he did.

"I'm just saying. I know you signed the contract to be brought into this, and yeah, they're going to be filming pretty much everything on this trip. But that doesn't mean you have to sacrifice yourself. You still have boundaries. You get to enforce them."

She was quiet for a moment, and for a second, he thought she might thank him. Or argue.

Instead, she tilted her head and said lightly, "I only want one, no filming in my bedroom. It may give people the wrong idea about other uses for that camera equipment... unless you're into that kind of stuff."

The shift was so fast it nearly gave him whiplash. Just like that, she'd gone from bracing for emotional collapse to weaponizing charm like a shield. And damn if it didn't work.

A grin tugged at his mouth before he could stop it. He rubbed a hand through his hair.

How does she do that?

"That's fine," he said, catching her gaze with a mock-serious wink. "We'll just do any bedroom filming in my room."

It was fascinating to watch it be her turn to blush. Her fair skin, dotted with a million freckles, showed her blush move from her face and down to her neck and chest as well. She looked away. She was a very expressive person; the camera was going to love her.

She was sitting with her feet in the water, legs swishing back and forth. Looking like a retro postcard that reminded him of Rita Hayworth.

As she stretched her arms over her head. Still working out the stiffness that came with being cooped up on a plane for too long. He could feel his pulse quicken at the sight.

"I'm sure you, Brent, and DeMarcus will have a lot of fun with that."

He laughed out loud. She had no filter, and it was so refreshing.

Maybe when this was all over, he could see where this spark of theirs could lead. Maybe if he could pull off a smooth investigation. Maybe they would get lucky enough to find Reagan and reunite her with Diana. That was a lot of maybes, he thought wistfully. However, maybe it could be the start of something beautiful here.

He heard car doors, and it meant the guys were back from their errands. He helped DeMarcus bring in the giant whiteboard, while Diana, with a cover-up on now, helped Brent bring in the groceries and put everything away.

While he and DeMarcus set up the living room up to be their studio. He could hear Diana and Brent chatting in the kitchen. He couldn't really make out what they were saying, but he could tell by her tone she was talking happily and not stewing as she had been on the plane.

"So, what's up with you and her?" DeMarcus asked lowly.

"What do you mean?

"She had you laughing. On the plane. And well, you don't laugh like that a lot."

"She's got a good sense of humor. She's honestly using it as a coping mechanism. I'm pretty sure she's just trying not to think about why she's here too much."

"And neither are you. She's gonna hate you by the end of this."

"Don't all the pretty women?" He muttered, a grim sensation spreading through him.

Guilt at not telling her everything he knew was still gnawing at him.

He should have said something when they'd been by the pool, but he'd been distracted.

That was one thing he hadn't prepared for when he invited her. That she was going to be this much of a distraction. Or that he'd care so much about the outcome of the case, knowing it could affect any future he may have potential for with Diana.

Push too hard, ask embarrassing or sensitive questions, shine light on a truth she doesn't want aired. So many of those things typically happen, and all end with the same result. Her never wanting to see him again.

Hopefully, it didn't come to having to choose Diana or the truth. He thought wistfully. Full well knowing how these investigations typically went, that it always does. Because we all have something to hide.

****

The next morning went by in a rush. Diana got up and made breakfast for the crew, since she wasn't sure she trusted their cooking skills. Eggs, bacon, sausage, and biscuits. It was easy enough to do. It was something to keep her mind off the day.

Now she was dressed, ready for the morning interview. She brought a spiral notebook with tabs to help keep her on track for the case and was wearing an outfit she typically wore to work. A pink button-down silk shirt and charcoal pants.

Figured since she was going to be on TV, looking feminine and professional would make sure her grandmother wasn't rolling in her grave about being presentable. Or making a bad impression on the cops they would be meeting later.

They put the whiteboard in front of the fireplace and set up a card table with chairs for their interview and notes.

Brent was hovering behind DeMarcus, who set up a couple of cameras. One to focus on her face, one to focus on Sam's face, and one for a wide angle that included the entire room and the whiteboard.

There, they had taped up the pictures he'd shown her previously and the timeline of her last days. There was a big question mark written above the word suspect. Next to the last picture he'd shown her during the first interview.

Since the interview wasn't really going to have the option for reshoots, being able to capture each moment from different angles was important.

Sam was once again ready with her lapel mic and stepped forward to help her. The button-down shirt worked much better this time, though if she'd been thinking ahead, she might have worn an undershirt.

Judging by the way his eyes flickered down, then quickly away. Just a little too fast. It seemed he might've appreciated the oversight.

"Sorry," he murmured, his voice low as his fingers brushed her collarbone, threading the cord around her back.

She didn't respond. Her heart thumping so loudly she was sure they'd be able to hear it.

Then, just like that, his expression snapped back into business mode.

DeMarcus gave the thumbs up, and it was time to start.

"Welcome back to Second Look Cases, a True Crime Podcast. I am your host, Sam Benson, and with me today is Diana Ramsey. Last time we sat down with her, we had broken the news that it now seems very unlikely that her niece, child internet sensation Reagan Ramsey, had run away. It is more likely that Reagan is actually missing under very suspicious circumstances."

He paused for a breath, then continued

"You've had a few days to process that. How are you feeling now that you're in L.A. and we're gonna work to get her case re-investigated?"

"I'm eager to get started. I appreciate y'all for letting me come with you. I promise to earn my keep on this trip and get to the truth. No matter how horrible it may be."

"That is very brave of you to say. However, what would you say to the people who feel like you are just trying to redeem yourself from the lack of responsibility you felt towards your niece when she originally went missing?"

So we are starting this right out of the gate. Diana thought to herself before she responded. She'd been prepared for that. She'd spent more time watching his interview style and knew he liked to throw hardball questions at the beginning of interviews to throw people off.

"To fuck off, honestly. Until you've walked in my shoes, it's easy to Monday morning quarterback life. Hindsight is always 20/20. I am here now, and I'm not going home without answers."

He barely contained his smile at that comment. Getting to know him better on that plane ride gave him more emotional heartstrings to pull at. But it also gave her an insight into him as well.

"What questions are you most hoping to get answered today when we talk to the police?" He asked, going to the next question on his clipboard.

"My hope? Is that she is alive and well. That they know where she is, and you just wasted all this money and podcast time for nothing."

He had to look away from the camera to hide his smile.

Diana thought to herself, Sam 0 - Diana 2.

But he quickly recovered and followed up with.

"And what is your greatest fear you may learn from the police?"

Diana took a deep breath. Again, this was something she expected to be asked at some point. But it didn't lessen the gnawing fear that it could be true. That feeling was painfully eating away at her heart.

"That...she's gone." That should be pretty obvious. But it really hurt to put those words out there. As if saying it was a possibility meant it was true.

"Gone as in dead?"

Diana nodded. "As long as she's missing, there is hope."

His eyes were filled with empathy. But he could keep a mostly stern face. Then he looked away, and she got the distinct feeling that him not meeting her eye in this moment meant something bad was about to happen.

"So, the timeline, as you know it currently, is that she filmed a skit at the Santa Monica Pier. And the next morning her mom woke up to find her missing and the money from her accounts withdrawn."

Diana gave him a puzzled look. The way he phrased that meant something was up... She eyed him suspiciously. "Yes, that is what I was told."

"We found evidence that the skit filmed at Santa Monica Pier was from the week prior, not the day before. That was just when they posted it."

"What?"

Anger infused her tone. His face was full of emotion, and regret was the chief one of them.

"Yes, and that's not all we found. This is the last recording of Reagan, and it was never released."

He handed her a tablet, and she watched.

Reagan was riding in a car, going down a highway past several exit signs. The trees didn't look like the trees she'd passed on the way from the airport;

they were...greener, fuller.

She was lip syncing to music, but she never showed the driver. Something was off about her; there was no smile in her eyes. And her pupils looked dilated.

She was lip syncing, so she couldn't tell if she was slurring her words, but she looked off somehow.

Diana wiped away tears and restarted the video, looking for clues. As heartbreaking as it was in the moment. She was eager to see Reagan in a new video. But now was not the time for those feelings. She needed to focus on what was useful.

"These trees, they look different. This wasn't around here, was it?" She said after a deep breath. Putting a lid on her rioting emotions.

"That's a good observation. Can you describe what the video is to the audience?"

"A road trip. She's lip syncing to Katy Perry's California Gurls." She recognized the song.

"And you noticed the trees. What about them makes them look different from the ones around here?"

"They're bigger, greener. Right now, everything here looks dry."

"What else do you notice about the video?" He asked.

"Her eyes are dilated, and although I can't hear her voice, she seems out of it. Like if I could, her speech would be slurred. I'm thinking she's under the influence." What had they been doing to her?

"That's right, folks. Diana is spot on with what our experts determined from the cursory look at this video, too. There's a chance the police already have this evidence, but this is what we'll be bringing to them today, along with the picture from our anonymous source."

"Wait, I'm confused. If the police already had this evidence, why would she still be listed as a runaway?"

"That is a great question. We'll make sure we ask them."

"Why didn't they talk to the friend who filmed with her at Santa Monica Pier about when that video was taken?"

"It sounds like you have all the right questions to ask. Are you ready to go ask them?"

"No shit, Sherlock! It's what I'm here for. You're the one who wanted to do this part first...next time, we'll chat it in the car for your fluff pieces."

"Deal." He said with a smile as he stood up.

He made a motion to DeMarcus to cut the filming, and then turned back to Diana.

"You did great. Grab your stuff and we'll head to the station right away."

"Why didn't you show me this before?" She was trying very hard not to yell at him or throw in the word asshole at the end of her sentence. But she could hear the frustration in her tone, and she hoped he felt it.

"Honestly? It felt cruel to keep going on Friday," Sam said, quieter than before. "And I knew it would only be a few days until we were here, sharing more. I didn't want you to... I didn't want you to back out."

Her frustration snapped. "What on earth gave you that idea? Just say it. It was for shock value. For views." She stepped forward, eyes blazing. "And going forward? Don't assume I'm gonna balk at anything I need to do to find Reagan. So you can take that bullshit excuse and shove it."

He looked surprised to see how angry she was... he really shouldn't be. It was a lousy excuse.

"Yes, ma'am," He said defensively with his hands up.

She looked over at DeMarcus and Brent, and both were grinning at her turns of phrases, but they quickly left to head to the police station.

And Diana wondered. How could a guy who was so adamant about the truth be so selective with the truth when it benefited him?

Chapter 7

They kept filming in the car, even though not much was being said. Diana kept her head down. Silently praying they could get answers at the police station.

"Hi, we're here to see Detective Diaz," Sam said to the officer behind the counter.

Diana noticed he looked a little young, considering the rank he wore. She also couldn't help but notice he looked like a Greek god and wondered briefly if all the cops in L.A. looked like movie stars.

"You're gonna have to be more specific," he responded.

"Detective Ashley Diaz. She's the lead investigator on the Reagan Ramsey missing persons case." Sam said.

Diana was a little startled by how this conversation was unfolding. So businesslike, so boring. It would not get them anywhere. He was making it too easy for the officer to say no and delay their investigation.

"And who are you?" he asked, looking bored.

"I'm Sam Benson, from Second Look Cases, the true crime podcast. This is Reagan's aunt Diana." He said with a gesture in her direction.

"Did you make an appointment?"

Sam hesitated, looking expectantly at Brent.

"I didn't think we'd need one." Brent piped up.

Diana had had enough. They were chasing their tails with the Desk Sergeant.

"Guys, go sit down. I'll handle this," Diana said, pointing to the bench on the far wall of the lobby.

"But..." Sam started.

She pointed again for emphasis until they complied.

"I'm so sorry, sir. What is your name?" She put the extra sugar into her southern accent. While they had been looking at Brent, she had popped open an extra button on her shirt. It wasn't scandalous, just strategic.

"Uhhh. I'm Sgt. Wickham. Ma'am, I'm sorry to hear about your niece."

Diana was truly touched by the thoughtfulness of that comment. It also gave her a clue that she was right in how she needed to approach this situation.

"Thank you. You're honestly the first person to say that since these guys showed up on my doorstep in South Carolina asking about her."

He shook his head. She leaned a little on the counter. She could tell his eyes caught sight of her cleavage, and he shifted on his feet.

"What part of South Carolina?" He asked, his entire demeanor changing to a more positive one.

"Pawleys Island. It's between Myrtle Beach and Charleston."

"I know it well. I was a Marine at Parris Island for a while." He said with a warm smile.

Diana could catch the slight southern accent that entered his voice.

Yes! She thought. Maybe it's a culture thing, but in the south it's normal to do a little chit chatting before you get down to business.

"That's awesome. Thank you for your service." Diana knew she'd gotten him on her side.

"Thank you for your support. So what happened to your niece?" He asked.

"I was always told she ran away. Then these guys showed up with new evidence, and it now seems like something more sinister happened."

She hated how this came out like an excuse, because the guilt twisting her stomach told her she should have come to L.A. sooner.

"I didn't get a chance to be involved much when it happened. My mom had a stroke, and I was her full-time caregiver. But with this new evidence, we really need to show it to Detective Diaz and get another look at everything."

"What kind of evidence?"

She explained what Sam had revealed to her so far.

"I am sorry to hear that, ma'am. I will, of course, get Detective Diaz. It may take a bit. I know right now she's preparing for a homicide trial."

"We completely understand. You know, we had some other people we could talk to if she's busy. Since the crew over there isn't as good at respecting other people's schedules. I'll make sure we work with hers." She said, handing him a card with her number on it.

"Sure thing, ma'am, just hold tight, and I'll see if she can step away for a bit and talk to you since you came all this way."

Diana thought he was a nice guy. A little standoffish to the others, because no cop enjoyed talking to someone they thought was from the media. But with her treating him like a person, not just a uniform. It helped.

"Thank you, Sergeant. I don't know what they're paying you out here, but you deserve a raise."

And with that, he got on the phone, and Diana walked over to where the guys were sitting.

DeMarcus had still been filming and had a goofy grin on his face. Brent and Sam looked dumbfounded.

"Did you just give your number to that guy?" Sam asked, a little more sternly than she thought the situation called for.

So she stood directly in front of where he was sitting and refasten the button she'd popped open right at his eye level.

"You get more flies with sugar than vinegar, and you're welcome."

"And where did that accent come from?" Sam asked.

"I'm from the south. It gets worse when I talk to other southerners."

"Listen, I'm not paying for this trip for you to go on dates with fucking Hercules over there. This is a work trip, one for your missing niece. Remember?"

Diana was shocked at his tone.

"Are you fucking kidding me right now? I'm not going on a date with him unless he can get me access to the information I need. Right now, we don't know what we need. Other than friends. Friends with resources. Friends willing to run a tag for us, or submit paperwork for a warrant. I always make friends at the police department. Hell, you met one. Remember Ray?"

"Did you show him your tits, too?"

He muttered it under his breath, not realizing Diana had excellent hearing. Her head snapped around the second the words left his mouth. Shocked, he

65

said something so immature.

The look on his face said it all: wide eyes, jaw slack, horrified that he'd actually said it out loud.

It took every ounce of willpower Diana had not to punch him in the face. She wanted to.

But then she'd get arrested. And then where would she be?

However, she didn't have to sit next to him. She would go outside and plot her revenge until the nice Sergeant Wickham let her know if they could see Detective Diaz today or not.

She didn't say a word. She just got up and walked out.

She heard Sam yell, "Dammit, come back here", but she didn't stop. She made it to the front steps and took in a deep breath.

She heard the doors open behind her and decided to keep moving down the stairs to the sidewalk.

She was a fast walker. She kept going, just shy of jogging. Her anger giving her momentum through a crowd of pedestrians.

A hand grabbed her shoulder, and she whirled to face him. Except it wasn't Sam. It looked like a homeless man had jumped out of the bushes and was holding a knife. She could see Sam still trying to make his way through the crowd, but he was too far away to help.

Instinct took over.

The homeless man yelled, "Give me your wallet, red."

She stepped to the side and grabbed his wrist, and twisted the joint back to control the weapon. Elbowing him in the face at the same time and then prying the knife free. She then armbarred him to the ground and stamped a foot on his face. So that he was essentially immobilized.

The man was too stunned to move.

Sam was running now. Clearly in a panic, but wasn't sure what to do by the time he got to her.

"What the fuck!" he yelled. Brent and DeMarcus were not far behind.

"You tried to rob the wrong motherfucker." Diana yelled at the homeless man.

She wasn't angry at the homeless man, who was likely just trying to survive.

All the anger she felt was for Sam. Who had bungled this meeting before it ever started, then appeared jealous when she had to resort to some creative tactics to fix it. And had the audacity to demand the truth, but gave nothing in return, after keeping the timeline information secret from her for days.

Whatever good will their conversation on the plane and that night at the bar had gained was gone. This guy was a joke. He clearly had no clue what he was doing and was likely just gonna ruin her life.

"Go get the Sergeant." She yelled at them.

"Give me the knife," Sam said.

His voice was tight. Low. Just this side of a command.

Diana heard it, but she was too keyed up to care.

"No," she snapped. "I've got this. See this? This is what handling business looks like."

She didn't miss the savage flicker in his eyes.

"It may be a novel experience to you," she said, twisting the knife into his male ego. "Not setting up an appointment with the detective? You're a fucking amateur. And I will not let you run Reagan's case into the ground with your fucking incompetence."

His nostrils flared. Just slightly. A muscle in his cheek twitched.

She had hit a nerve. His spine locked straight, and for a heartbeat, she thought he might grab her. She saw the instinct flash through his posture. The way his feet planted and his shoulders squared. The protector in him was screaming to act.

"I think you're overreacting," he said finally. His voice forced to sound calm and reasonable. But she could hear the barely restrained anger in it as well. "If you'd given me a second, I would've told you, I do book appointments normally. Brent handles logistics now. That's why he's here. So I can focus on the case."

His hands were clenched at his sides.

"And I'm sorry about the tits comment. It caught me off guard. You flirting, using your looks to get answers. It just surprised me."

"The master manipulator can't recognize another master?" she snapped.

He stepped closer. And this time, he didn't stop himself from towering over her.

"I've never used my looks to get anything out of anyone," he growled. "I use facts. Evidence."

"Bullshit," she spat. "Look at you right now. Looming over me, trying to get me to comply with your wishes with just your body language."

He blinked. Once. Then his voice dropped again, colder this time.

"You think I'm trying to intimidate you? If I were, you wouldn't be standing here talking." There was a warning in his tone.

The tension between them snapped taut. Even the air felt different, like lightning waiting to strike.

"I don't work for you," she shot back, not flinching. "You have no authority over me. So I can say what I want, do what I want, and go out with whoever the hell I want."

A beat. His jaw flexed. Then the homeless man made a half-assed attempt to struggle from her grasp.

"Don't even think about it," Sam growled to the man, who quickly stopped moving again.

Sergeant Wickham came running up the street.

"This man tried to rob me with a knife," Diana yelled out to him.

She kept him in the armbar, and didn't let off of his face until the handcuffs were on. Once he was secure, she handed the knife over to the Sergeant.

"Are you ok?" he asked.

"See, Sam, this is how you treat a lady. Yes, Sergeant, I'm fine, thank you." She said, not looking at the Sergeant, but at Sam. Twisting that knife in his male ego just a little more.

Sam stormed off.

"He has it bad, huh?" The Sergeant said with a smile. Suggesting the tension between them was more than professional.

Diana didn't smile back. She was pissed, and yes, he was attractive, but Reagan's case meant more to her than a hot guy.

"Doesn't really matter. I just met that guy a few days ago." Diana said, dismissing Sam from her thoughts as she focused on the adrenaline dump that was hitting her body. Her hands were starting to shake.

"Well, good news is Detective Diaz can meet with y'all in about 30 min-utes. In the meantime, let's get this guy booked, and I'll get your witness statement."

"You, sir, are a gentleman."

Chapter 8

Sam stormed down the sidewalk in the opposite direction of Diana.

"What the hell has gotten into you?" Brent said, catching up.

"YOU! ASSHOLE! Why didn't you book the appointment, Brent?" Sam yelled at him, losing his temper.

"Hey, I'm not the one who commented on her tits. Or acted like a jealous boyfriend. To a woman you didn't even know existed days ago. What the hell happened?"

Sam stopped and ran a hand through his hair. Brent was right. He was acting like an immature asshole.

"I just thought she was different, I thought..."

His neatly laid plan of impressing her with a smooth investigation. Reuniting her with her niece. He wanted to be like a knight in shining armor, so he could investigate that spark. All went up in smoke at the way she behaved with the desk sergeant. And the way he responded to her behavior? It was with the most insensitive comment his idiotic brain could come up with. Was she playing him? Trying to get him to go easy on her in the interviews? Would she just lie to him like all the others?

"What? That she liked you?" Brent asked.

"I don't know, maybe?"

"Of course, she likes you. All the girls like you."

Then why do they all lie and leave? He couldn't help but ask himself.

"You need to get your shit together. This is going to be an emotional roller coaster. We do not need you acting like a lovesick puppy every time she bats her big, beautiful eyes to get her way in this investigation."

The disappointment that had surged through him when he heard the accent, saw the shirt, and watched her egging the guy on had evaporated the second he saw her in trouble. It had been replaced instantly by panic and fear that he wouldn't get there in time to save her.

Then came the shock. She'd taken down a fully grown man with a knife like it was nothing. Like swatting away a bee that dared to get too close.

It was beautiful. And it was terrifying.

"I did my research on her very thoroughly. This was why I recommended inviting her. On the surface, yes, she looks like a sweet, innocent insurance agent. A damsel in distress, if you will. But that lady is no damsel. I don't know if they're just built differently in the south, or if there are more layers to her than you realize. I knew watching you find them out was going to make for a great show. Remember that's why we had to piece-meal the evidence drops. We don't want to overwhelm her... or the audience. We need them to want to keep tuning back in each episode."

Brent looked so damn proud of himself. Like a spider admiring the threads of his web as everything fell neatly into place.

"No, right now, I don't even know if we have a show. She seems about ready to pull the plug on everything." Sam said, kicking himself for how off the rails they were.

"After the interview, I'm gonna go back to the house to get started on the teaser release," Brent suggested.

Sam nodded. "And make sure you reach out to everyone else on the interview list. We'll get started tomorrow. I don't think we're gonna get much else today. Hopefully, she'll still be up for Bailey Jessica this afternoon."

"Sounds good. Well, let's make sure the interview with Diaz goes great."

They headed back to the lobby, but Diana wasn't there. He could see her in an office behind Sergeant Wickham's desk. He also saw they were still smiling and standing too close together as he helped her fill out her witness statement.

DeMarcus had followed her and was still filming from outside the door. Sam motioned for him to cut.

"Dude. I got the take-down on camera." He told Sam and Brent.

"Really?" Brent said excitedly.

"Yeah. Man, this chick is badass."

A beautiful Latina detective entered the room with Wickham and Diana. Sam figured that must be Diaz.

He got up and headed for the office so they could capture the full interaction.

He tapped on the door before barging in with Brent and DeMarcus, hot on his heels.

"Excuse me, are you Detective Diaz, the one in charge of the Reagan Ramsey case?"

"Yes. Hey, I know you. You're Sam Benson!" She said excitedly.

"You've heard of me?" He was surprised.

"Yes. You interviewed my old Training Officer. He's in Chicago now. It was a story you did about the rumor of a serial killer operating in the area. They call him the Smiley Face Killer."

"Captain Davis, yes, I remember him."

"You did a great job on that article. It's not often we see a reporter actually being fair to law enforcement. Thank you for that."

"Thank you. Although honestly, I just call things like I see them. But, yeah, that was an interesting case."

"So is this one, from what I heard from Wickham."

"Yes, we came to show you what we uncovered," Sam responded. Brent handed him the folder.

They had taken over the office, and Diana and Wickham had stopped working on her report to listen in.

"The reason we wanted to talk to you was the Reagan Ramsey Case. She went missing five years ago. This is her aunt. And she can confirm, up till recently, the story had always been Reagan ran away." Sam said with a nod in Diana's direction.

"I seem to have anonymous sources in the FBI ICAC unit. They're swamped naturally, but this agent recognized Reagan in this photo because their daughter was a fan. They mentioned they couldn't get anyone to investigate further, because she was listed as a runaway." Diaz nodded like she wasn't surprised to hear that.

"Then I did an interview recently about what case I was taking next, and had casually mentioned this one as a possibility. The next morning, I woke up and boom. This is in my email."

He passed her the blurred photo.

"They tried to keep as much detail as possible because Reagan's case is unique. She's been missing for 5 years. Where she passed the age of 18. So determining when this photo was taken is critical to build a case against the man in the photo."

"We believe it's this man." He said, pulling out the second photo of the group of child actors from her videos, posing with the group of sponsors.

"We were told the last thing Reagan did was visit the Santa Monica Pier with her co-star Bailey Jessica. Then she came home, went to bed, and was gone by morning. Except when we watched the video from the pier, they passed this Churro Cart. He's got a date on his menu board about a special for that day. That's from a week prior." Sam said as he sorted through more evidence in his folder to lay out.

"So we went hunting for that missing week. We found Reagan's old manager had passed away. But he had a storage unit going up for auction. So, on a hunch, we bought it. Hoping it would have evidence. We struck gold. We found the login information to Reagan's YouTube account." They all looked at him with surprise. He agreed it was like looking for a needle in a haystack and finding it.

"That's where we found one last unpublished video."

He pressed play on the video and pointed out the timestamp was two days before she was reported missing. Diaz leaned in to watch it over his shoulder.

"Ok, we saw this. It was part of the initial investigation. But her mom said it was a trip to see the redwoods in northern California. That it was from two days before her disappearance. And she was back in LA to film the Pier thing the day before."

"Layla was a compulsive liar. I wouldn't believe anything she told you," Diana said.

"Yeah, it seems like there was never any movement on the case since that first year. And I'll be honest, it was never that high of a priority because, unlike most runaways, Reagan had the means to take care of herself with the money she took." Diaz commented, looking sympathetically at Diana.

"Like I said, don't trust Layla. Are you sure she took the money?" Diana insisted.

Diaz rummaged through her case file but audibly sighed when it didn't include a bank statement.

"No, I believe the original detective took her at her word."

"Ok, what happens next?" Diana asked.

"How long y'all in town for?" Diaz asked.

"I know I was hoping to be here no more than 2 weeks. That's when I have to get back to work," Diana replied.

"We can be at your disposal indefinitely," Sam said. Gesturing to himself and his crew.

"I'm in the middle of a homicide trial. A mother killed her husband for molesting their daughter, so it's a real shit show. I don't know how long it'll take. There's a good chance jury selection itself will take half the time you're here for."

"I can help," Wickham announced.

Diaz still looked skeptical about the podcasters inserting themselves into her case. Sam noticed.

"Most of what we're doing is retracing the work you've already done," Sam assured her.

"Before we touch anything that might lead into fresh territory, we'll come to you. The goal is to raise awareness, not jeopardize the integrity of a future prosecution."

Diaz gave a small nod, still guarded. "Fine. Keep me in the loop with any progress. If this case goes to a plea deal, it'll wrap up quickly. Then I'll be able to give you more time."

"California is a weird place. Y'all prosecute someone we'd give a high five to where I'm from." Diana mentioned.

Diaz's mouth twitched into a bit of a smile at that, but she kept silent.

"So if you can follow the money, Pete. We wanted to talk to Bailey Jessica and see if there is anything she didn't share with the police. It looks like y'all already talked to her." Diana said, pointing at the witness statement visible from the case file.

Sam looked around. Who was Pete?

"Sure, here, hand me your phone and I'll program my number in for you," Wickham said, hand extended.

Diana gave him a bright smile and passed the phone over without hesitation.

That stabbing sensation hit Sam again. Sharp. Same place as before. Watching her with Wickham like they'd known each other for years.

Brent had called it jealousy. Maybe it was. Or maybe it was the slow crush of hope under the weight of a single unfiltered sentence. The one that made her walk away and into danger. That was the part that was unforgivable to the standard Sam typically held himself to. She'd almost gotten hurt because of him.

Detective Diaz rolled her eyes at the interaction, but Sam focused on gathering the folder of evidence in his hands. She handed him her business card. Her personal number was scribbled across the back. A slight gesture, but Diana caught it.

Sam saw the flicker in her expression. Barely there. But real. And just like that, something shifted in him. The spark wasn't just his imagination. Whatever tension buzzed between them. She felt it too. He just had to find the right way to redeem himself for his stupidity.

Detective Diaz was a beautiful woman with dark hair and eyes. She honestly looked like a Disney Princess. Who was he kidding? He could barely keep his eyes off of Diana. Her freckled face, pointed chin, and long red hair down to her elbows. It was probably obvious to everyone in the room that he couldn't hide how smitten he was with her.

"Was there any other evidence that stuck out in this case we don't know about?" He asked, accepting the card and putting it in his pocket.

"It was noted there was a good relationship with her grandmother, which was well known to her friends. A lot of them thought she would show up in South Carolina. I'm guessing y'all never heard from her?"

"No, Mom had a stroke the same day she was reported missing, and it left her with aphasia. She wasn't really able to communicate after that," Diana said sadly. And Sam felt the urge to comfort her with a small squeeze on her shoulder.

"Well, now that we know we're not looking for her on a yacht somewhere, we may finally make some progress," Wickham said.

"Thank you for meeting with us, and thank you, Sergeant, for stepping up to help. You have no idea how much I appreciate it." Diana said, shaking both of their hands as they headed to the lobby.

"So we're gonna drop Brent off at the house. He's gonna start working on the teaser for the episode while the three of us go have lunch with Bailey Jessica. She's a student at UCLA and should be done with classes now. I set up the interview," Sam said loudly, mostly so Diana could hear him as they approached the rental.

He tried to find the right words.

"You guys, go ahead and start the car. I want to talk to Diana," he said, handing the keys to DeMarcus.

"But I don't want to talk to you."

She turned to get in the car.

Sam reached out, catching her arm. Not hard, just enough to make her pause. He knew the move was risky. She could drop him just like she had that guy on the sidewalk. But he had to say it.

"I'm sorry," he said, voice low. "That whole thing, what I said. You deserved better. Reagan deserved better. You have my word. The rest of this investigation will go as smoothly as we can make it."

She didn't look at him. The moment dragged on.

Sam let out a breath he'd been holding. He let go of her arm.

She got into the car without a word. The silence rattled him more than if she'd yelled. More than if she'd slapped him. Diana was a fighter. The fact that she wasn't fighting at all?

That scared him the most. Because it meant she thought there was nothing worth fighting for.

Chapter 9

Diana told the guys she was just going to freshen up, as they were doing a quick stop just to drop Brent off.

She walked straight to her room, not looking at any of them. She closed the door behind her and sat on the bed. Then she picked up the pillow and screamed into it.

She let out all the bottled-up frustration into that pillow. The anger, the hurt, the feeling of being let down.

Sam showed her a side of him that just yesterday she wouldn't have thought even existed. He was ruthless and a bit grim and grumpy. But that comment felt borderline misogynistic. Was he used to charming all the female interviewees and having them fawn over him like Detective Diaz did when she realized who he was?

Not that she was jealous... really. She told herself. It just rubbed her the wrong way for him to say what he did, only to have the little Miss Bambi eyes drooling over him 5 minutes later. He likely had tons of women doing that to him regularly. But she refused to be one of them.

Her plan to keep things purely professional was smart. Hopefully, before she had to return to work, the case would be solved and she would never have to see him again.

There was a knock at her door.

"GO AWAY!" she yelled.

"It's me. Can I talk to you?"

She was surprised to hear DeMarcus's voice.

He was the youngest person on the crew and, so far, it seemed the most competent. Plus, he seemed to be a sweet kid.

Diana sat up on the bed and took a deep breath.

"Only if it's you. And no cameras," she called out.

"It's only me." He said with his hands up.

He walked closer to where she sat on the bed with the pillow. It was something she had done since she was a teenager, when her dad had refused to continue the cancer treatments and her life had spiraled out of control as he got sicker and sicker. And she hadn't wanted him to see how much pain his choice not to fight had caused her.

"I wanted to apologize."

"For what? From what I can see, you've done nothing wrong, and they should let you be in charge. Clearly, you're the smart one."

"I appreciate that. I just wanted to give some context. See, I know Sam. He may have mentioned my mom is his accountant, but it's more than that. We lived next door to him when everything went down with his ex-wife."

"Ok, and? If we're comparing sob stories, I'll give him a run for his money."

"Well, since then, he's not been the same. Not only did he lose her, his job, and his best friend. He kind of lost his mind there for a while, and has thrown himself into work ever since."

"And your point is?" Diana asked.

"What do you think his work is?"

"Being an asshole."

DeMarcus smiled.

"No, it's a lot of late nights doing research, talking to people who lie to him constantly, all while being a performing monkey for the masses. He doesn't go out to have fun. It's all about networking, or chasing leads."

"Are you saying that all work and no play have made Jack a dull boy?... Wait, you may be too young for that reference. Please continue." She said with a hand gesture for him to hurry up and get to the point.

"Basically, and I actually got that reference, The Shining is a classic. I think he likes you, and that's weird and scary for him. I haven't heard him laugh or be playful like he did on the plane since before his divorce."

She got the feeling DeMarcus was rooting for them to become a thing. Which, yesterday, would have been almost sweet. Today... no chance in hell, buddy.

"I don't want him to like me. I just want to get through this. Yes, we had a nice plane ride, yes, he's an attractive man, yes, if we met under different circumstances, things may be different. But I also live in the real world. And in the real world, I live in South Carolina, and he lives... actually, I don't know where he's based out of."

"DC still." DeMarcus supplied.

"DC, whatever, point's the same. If he wants me to give him any usable content, he needs to remain professional. I give what I get. It's been my thing my whole life. And you can warn him. I can go from Southern Charm to Trailer Trash in about 5 seconds flat if he ever says a comment like that again. Beth Dutton doesn't have shit on what I would do to him."

"Yes ma'am, I caught that reference too."

"Good," Diana said with a nod for emphasis.

"I think we're ready to go if you are."

"Sure, let's get this over with."

Diana stood up and grabbed her bag with her notebook. She would write all the questions she wanted to ask Bailey and continue to ignore Sam until the urge to throw things at his head subsided. At least he had apologized to her at the first moment he could.

She could tell he was sincere and heard the care in his voice. Which had lessened her rage quite a bit when he stopped her at the car, but the urge to twist that knife into his male ego was still present, and she'd let him stew a bit longer so they could hopefully focus more on the case.

"I stand by what I said. They should let you be in charge."

He gave her a quick grin at that.

"I keep telling my little sister Tasha that, but she never believes me."

They left Brent to begin the editing for the episode and drove to the UCLA campus.

Diana sat quietly in the front passenger seat. Choosing to look out of the window at the passing scenery rather than engage with Sam or DeMarcus, even though he was still filming her.

It was causing a noticeable rise in the tension that she could tell was affecting Sam the way he would glance at her, and then away, with his hands tightening on the steering wheel.

"Listen, I am really sorry about what I said at the police station. It was completely out of line." He said finally. Reiterating his apology from earlier.

Diana looked pointedly at DeMarcus, who was filming.

"You will be sorry," was all Diana gave him.

Sam looked at DeMarcus and visibly grimaced.

"Can't we just have a moment, kid?"

DeMarcus nodded and stopped filming.

"I'm sorry, I have no filter. Whatever comes into my head generally has a good chance of coming out of my mouth, too."

"Really, Mr. No Filter? Then why were you jealous?" Diana asked directly. He didn't answer.

"See, I think you were jealous because I got answers when you couldn't. You're so used to being the star, you felt upstaged."

When they hit a red light, Sam looked over at her, and this time, he didn't look away. His gaze lingered, drifting lower, slowly sweeping back up to meet her eyes again. It wasn't subtle. It was pure hunger. Diana started rethinking her assumption about why he was acting like a jealous boyfriend...maybe it wasn't professional jealousy.

The way he was looking at her now felt wolfish... and it was causing heat to curl her toes and her heart rate to jump, and her breathing to increase in anticipation. There was a very big urge to look away and blush, but she'd be damned if she let him win this battle.

They weren't alone. DeMarcus was very present in the back seat. That made him not say what was clearly on his face. It also made her choose her next words carefully and very quietly so only Sam could hear.

"Just stop, okay. This is not the time or the place to have this conversation. And truth be told, this conversation needs to not happen until we find Reagan. But at that point, you won't need me anymore for your podcast, and you'll be moving on to the next story." It was the most direct warning she could give him at this moment.

The long looks, the flirting that had come so naturally to them while in South Carolina needed to be put to the side while they were here. Because Reagan was the only thing that mattered.

Someone honked behind them as he had lingered at the now green light too long. They drove the rest of the way in silence.

They met up with Bailey Jessica outside the library and walked with her to her dorm.

After shaking Bailey's hand, Diana said, "It's nice to finally meet you."

The girl was beautiful, with long blonde hair, clear blue eyes. A real looker. No wonder the camera loved her. She and Reagan must've made a perfect contrast, light and dark, soft and sharp.

"Reagan talked about you a lot," Diana added, her tone warm but steady.

"Yeah, she loved visiting you guys," Bailey said. "I was always a little jealous. I didn't have a getaway spot to escape to like she did."

Just that one sentence made Diana's throat tighten. Someone else remembering Reagan fondly brought back so many memories, and the familiar ache of just missing her company.

"You're from Wisconsin, right? Must've been a big shift coming out here."

"Huge," Bailey said. "We had a dairy farm. I used to post chore videos. Feeding chickens, brushing cows, that kind of thing. One video of me getting chased by a rooster went viral."

"I saw that one," Diana said, a genuine smile curling up. "You were what, five?"

Bailey laughed. "Yup."

"How'd you end up working with Reagan?"

"We had the same manager."

There was more behind her eyes. Diana could see it, but before she could gently nudge it loose, Sam jumped in.

"You were one of the last people to see her, right?"

Bailey's body language shifted, shoulders pulling in slightly, eyes narrowing.

"Yeah. We went to the pier. There was an event for spring break, so it was packed. We loved people-watching, commenting on outfits, and filming dumb skits. Nothing serious."

"Do you remember the exact date?" Sam asked.

Another hesitation. Diana gave him a sideways glance, subtle, but clear. Ease up.

"You said it was like yesterday, spring break, a big event. But not the date?"

His tone was too sharp. Diana winced inwardly. She didn't want Bailey to clam up.

"April 13th," Bailey finally answered.

"But the video didn't post until the 18th. Why the delay?"

"Bruce, our manager, asked me to wait. He said something about fan safety. We were getting weird letters, and he didn't want people knowing where we were in real time. I stayed local that whole week, but Reagan went up north."

"With her mom?" Diana asked.

"Her mom's boyfriend booked a cabin. That's what she said, anyway."

Sam jotted notes. "These letters, did you see any of them?"

"No. Bruce kept them to himself. Said some were graphic, and he didn't want us stressing out.... why do you ask?"

Bailey Jessica was clearly very smart if she was starting to put the pieces together.

Diana took a breath.

"We don't think Reagan ran away."

Bailey stopped walking, mouth slightly open.

"What?"

Diana reached out, squeezing her shoulder gently, knowing the shock of realization that was hitting her.

"Sam found new evidence. Stuff I never knew. She was apparently hospitalized before. For a suicide attempt. Did you know that?"

Bailey's eyes went wide. Her expression cracked.

Diana heard herself asking too many questions, too fast.

She'd done the same thing Sam did. Dammit.

"Reagan was fine that day. It was just us and our camera guy, Hassan. So no parents, no managers, just us having a fun day." She said before taking a deep breath and continuing to walk so she could look at the ground and not at them or the camera.

"I knew about the attempt, but I don't know if the attempt is what I would call it. She liked to sneak out to parties and would take a lot of pills, not really caring what they were, or how many. Is that suicidal, or just being reckless?"

Diana nodded but stayed silent, hoping she would continue.

"She would just get out of control. I stopped going with her. I had promised my parents that I wouldn't let LA get to me like that. We'd seen too many horror stories of drugs, addiction, and this lifestyle could ruin people. I only did content creating to support my family. As soon as I made enough to pay off the family farm and make it through college, I quit. And I think that's the difference. I saw it as a job, not a lifestyle."

They arrived at the building where her dorm was.

"Thank you for talking to us. I know it was probably scary for you watching your friend put herself in harm's way like that," Diana said grimly.

Bailey nodded and wiped a tear from her eye.

"If you were us, where should we look next?" Diana thought to ask.

"Find out where this cabin in the woods was, and maybe there are clues there. Because that really is her last known location."

"Will do. Thank you so much for letting us come and get some context into Reagan's last days," Sam said, shaking her hand before Diana did the same.

"Yeah, anything to help her. She was such a sweet girl. I hope you find her." She said before turning to go inside.

Sam and Diana turned to DeMarcus with the camera and recapped what they learned.

They had been using a handheld mic, and Diana felt like a proper journalist now, talking into it while the camera was on her face.

"Now that we've talked to Bailey Jessica, how do you feel?" he asked her.

"Eager to head north and find this cabin," Diana replied. The wall was coming back up now that she was in front of the camera with Sam.

"And the information about Reagan sneaking out and doing drugs to the point people thought she was intentionally trying to harm herself?"

He seemed to know exactly where to twist the knife. Right in that part of her soul, eaten up with guilt about how little she knew about Reagan's life

"That is hard to hear, of course. It feels like a cry for help." The anger at herself made her voice tighten.

"A cry for help you never heard before today?" Sam pushed that knife just a little deeper.

"No, I did not know. But I do have a question for you."

"Really, go ahead?" he seemed surprised.

"She mentioned creepy letters. You said at the police station that you happened upon a storage unit sale of her manager's belongings. Did you find any of those letters Bailey mentioned? Could they be clues?"

"Sadly, no. It was mostly office furniture. The sticky note that had the login information had gotten wedged behind the drawer by accident; there were no other papers or files there."

"A fucking sticky note...wow." She was shocked.

He smiled at her. "Yeah, half of this case has been a series of lucky coincidences." And she couldn't help but reward him with a small smile herself.

He turned back to the camera to give a closing.

"We've confirmed the Pier video was shot the week before, and we now have a new lead on a cabin in the woods up north to investigate next. We'll meet up with our friends at the LAPD and see what they've turned up with the missing millions they've accused Reagan of taking, and see what happens next on Second Look Cases."

Chapter 10

When they returned to the car in the parking lot, they were surprised to see someone had parked an old 1990s Honda Civic behind their SUV and left it there. They couldn't get out. Sam pointed out that one tire was flat.

"I guess you'll just have to call a tow truck," Diana suggested

Sam nodded, but it was DeMarcus who made the call.

Sam clearly was hoping to have a moment alone with her, but Diana ignored the looks he was giving her. Instead, she texted Traci about their progress.

It wasn't long before the tow truck arrived, and they were on their way again.

As they sat in traffic. Diana noticed Sam kept checking the rear-view mirror. It was almost a compulsion.

"Why do you keep doing that?" She finally couldn't resist asking.

"I think we're being followed." He said.

Diana looked towards the mirror and saw a guy on a sport bike with a black helmet behind them, dressed all in black.

"The Motorcycle?" Diana wondered. Is this case related? Were they getting close enough to start making people responsible for Reagan's disappearance nervous?

"Yeah, he's been behind us ever since we left the college. If he were a student, he sure is driving far."

So, probably not a false alarm...was it possibly just someone looking to carjack them? Diana remembered reading an article about carjackings being on the rise in major cities.

"What are you going to do, blow the next red light or do a bunch of left turns?" Diana asked. Regardless if this was case related or just crime related, they needed a plan.

He looked at her as he rolled up to a red light and did the one thing she wasn't expecting.

He said "Stay here" and then he put the car in park and got out. Then preceded to walk back to where the guy was on the bike and questioned him.

Diana felt panic rising in her chest as she fumbled with her seat belt, and DeMarcus was hanging out of the rear seat window, blocking her side mirror's view of what was going on.

"This dumbass is trying to get himself killed." She muttered as she finally got the seat belt off and the door opened.

There was a sharp pang of fear that if he died because he had the dumb luck to start investigating this case over all the other ones. She would feel responsible.

She noticed Sam taking a picture of the guy's license plate as the rider was distracted by her getting out as well, and then they exchanged more words she couldn't hear.

"Thank you for the directions." Sam gave a forced smile and a wave to the biker as he was heading back to her.

"Get in the car, Diana." He said tersely. Grabbing her arm and dragging her back to the SUV.

"What's going on?" She asked.

He opened the door for her as she got back inside. Then he did a light jog to the driver's side.

As soon as the SUV started moving, the biker peeled off.

Sam let out a sharp breath, like he'd been holding it in. His knuckles were white on the steering wheel.

"Why didn't you stay in the damn car?" She could tell he was angry. It was a little surprising, since nothing seemed to have happened.

"Because you needed backup. Because you were running out there with no plan," she shot back.

His eyes flashed. "Diana, my job here is to keep you safe. Doing something

86

unexpected was the best way I could do that."

Diana scoffed

"I can keep myself safe. I'm pretty sure I proved that already."

"No. You got lucky. That's not the same thing." His forearms were tight, flexed.

Diana's temper got the better of her.

"Once again, don't use that holier-than-thou authoritarian tone with me." She stared at him, then added deliberately: "I. Don't. Work. For. You." Poking him in his bicep with each word...which was rock hard under her finger.

Sam slammed the brakes, the SUV jerking to a hard stop in the middle of traffic. Horns blared around them, but he didn't seem to care. Diana's temper was escalating to the point she was considering throwing hands. Or getting out of the vehicle and walking away.

He turned to her fully, eyes stormy. "That's enough. From here on out, if you pull another stunt like that, if you put yourself in harm's way again. I'm putting you on the first flight back to South Carolina. I mean it."

"Excuse the fuck outta me." Diana glared at him, incredulous. "Who the hell do you think you are?"

"I'm the guy trying to make sure you don't get killed," he snapped, the edge of panic just barely covered by frustration. "You think this is a game? That guy could've been anyone. Sent to hurt us. Sent to hurt you."

"So your 'plan' was just to go out there with no plan?" She countered.

"It's called breaking the OODA loop. If that guy was planning on doing us harm. He was likely waiting for us to get on the freeway so he could make a clean getaway. Stopping where I did. He was trapped and caught off guard by us doing something unexpected. It's not perfect, but it sounded better than letting him follow us to where there were fewer witnesses."

"Witnesses? That was your protection? How many times have there been attacks in broad daylight with no one helping them, because people don't want to get involved anymore? That is the most idiotic thing you could have said."

She knew he wasn't wrong about the OODA loop thing. It stood for Observe, Orient, Decide, and Act. It's a four-step approach to decision making that makes filtering information as quickly as possible in dynamic situations.

Hearing stories of soldiers throwing rubber duckies instead of flash-bangs while clearing rooms, because if someone was planning to do something, the sight of a rubber ducky would throw them off just enough to gain a tactical advantage.

But that worked better in military circles when you're playing offense. In the civilian world, you needed to think more defensively in your tactics. A prosecutor could look at his actions as starting an altercation, not as trying to avoid one.

If he'd just talked to her. Trusted her enough to come up with a plan. They could have handled the motorcyclist without either of them being in that much danger. She could see that Sam was considering her words as valid, but he refused to acknowledge them. Both of their tempers were triggered right now.

Diana took a deep breath. Remember Reagan. She needed his help to find Reagan.

Sam exhaled and shoved a hand through his hair and started driving again.

"What do you think, DeMarcus?" Diana said, hoping the kid would take her side and show Sam how stupid his non-plan of a plan was.

"I think you both make fair points. Dude, a little warning would have been nice, not gonna lie. However, Sam is effective at scaring people when he wants to. It seems to have worked. And that is, even if the guy was really trying to do something."

Sam nodded in the mirror at DeMarcus. Diana huffed.

Then Sam tossed his phone into her lap. "Send the plate number to your new boyfriend at the police department. See if he can run it for us."

Diana rolled her eyes. "Pete isn't my boyfriend. And you know you can't just have people run tags like that. It's illegal."

"I bet you $20 that if you ask, he'll do it," Sam said harshly.

"I bet you he won't." Diana retorted.

But she did as he asked and mentioned in her message that Sam thought he was following them for about 20 minutes since they left campus.

Sure thing. The reply came.

"Told you so."

Diana ignored him for the rest of the way to the house.

Just as they were walking inside, Pete responded.

That bike was reported stolen yesterday.

"Well, that's creepy." She said, showing Sam her phone. He said nothing, but went to hold the door to the house open for her and then locked it behind them. It was clear. He was taking no chances. Diana couldn't help but wonder if they were being followed because of the case, who was involved, and how did they get tipped off that they were investigating?

****

He'd been warned. She didn't want to explore the spark between them. She'd said as much to DeMarcus when he listened outside her door, and in the car. All because of his own stupid, unfiltered thought that had spilled from his mouth in a moment of weakness.

When did he get so unfiltered? He wondered.

Yelling at her about the motorcyclist probably didn't help either. But when he heard her door open and realized she'd stepped out, his stomach dropped like it never had before. That fear had been visceral.

The hair on the back of his neck had been standing up since he first noticed the motorcycle tailing them. He was sure it had to do with the case and wasn't random. And in the ten long minutes before she caught on, all he could come up with was his non-plan, plan, as she'd so helpfully called it.

He needed to accept the reality of her. She had an unpredictable, stubborn, and reckless nature. He needed to plan for that in the future. Because the truth was, he never knew what she'd do next. He hated that. And he loved it.

But more than anything, he needed her to trust him. Because when he acted to protect her, it couldn't be a fight every time. Goddamn, she was magnificent, but she wasn't invincible.

As they drove to meet Sergeant Wickham for dinner, it was all he could think about.

The more he got to know her, the more impressed he was. Not just personally, but professionally too. Watching her coax Bailey Jessica into opening up had transformed the entire interview. She got the girl to reveal things Sam was sure wouldn't have come out without Diana.

But also the way she maintained her composure when he asked about the new information learned. She was an intoxicating mix of strength and vulnerability. It had taken everything he had not to pull her into his arms when he noticed her lip tremble and her eyes well up at the cry for help comment.

He could only imagine how she was feeling. They knew it was going to be an emotional investigation for her, but this was the first time it affected him, too. Watching her handle all of this alone.

How long before they could go back to how they were on the plane, laughing and flirting and igniting a spark that had left him thinking he was going quickly from smitten to having a full-blown crush on the woman.

They pulled up to the restaurant Sergeant Wickham had recommended. He was no longer in his police uniform, but looking rather dapper in a black fitted long-sleeved shirt and pants that were tighter than they needed to be. And Sam had to remind himself she was just being nice to him to get information.

"Hi Pete!" she said, walking up to him outside the restaurant with a big smile.

She had also changed when they went back to the house to pick up Brent, who had finished the teaser and had it set to release at 9 pm that night. She was wearing a red wrap dress that cinched in at her waist and did wonders for her figure. He'd stopped breathing when he saw her coming out of her room in it.

"Hi Diana! You look lovely. I see you brought the whole gang…"

"Yep, just think of them as my three shadows." She said with a hint of sarcasm.

Sam rolled his eyes. This was gonna be a long night.

They got seated at their table, and Sam looked over the menu. They had a little bit of everything here, from steak to sushi to tacos.

"So, how did it go today?" Wickham asked.

"Great, we talked to Bailey Jessica, Reagan's co-star. She confirmed our suspicions about the timeline and mentioned a cabin up north that

Lalya's boyfriend had rented. I wanted to ask if y'all had a name or contact information for him. I keep hearing him being referenced, but I never knew him."

"Keith Novack. Not a really great guy. A couple of DUIs and an aggravated assault charge from when he was younger, from a bar fight .... I read over the entire file after you guys left today." Wickham mentioned.

"Do we know where he is?" Diana asked.

"Nope, that was another inconsistency I noticed. He hasn't been seen since Reagan's disappearance, but had never been reported missing either. I don't even think he was on the radar until Layla overdosed. When they were looking for where she may have gotten the bad drugs from. A neighbor had said an old boyfriend had turned up and identified Keith as the old boyfriend. There's just a giant chunk of missing years between when Reagan went missing and when Layla died."

"That's suspicious as hell," Sam said.

They all nodded.

"What kind of drugs?" Diana followed up with.

"Cocaine..it was laced with fentanyl." Wickham responded.

Diana shook her head.

They placed their orders and then waited for Wickham to mention what he'd found.

"So all the money Reagan made as a content creator had been put into a trust for her. She wasn't allowed to touch it until she was 18, which is pretty common for child stars. So she couldn't have taken the money."

That was another thing Layla had lied about, Sam thought.

"I also did my due diligence and went to the bank to see if they had security camera footage that went that far back. We got lucky, they kept them for 5 years, so we were days away from this being deleted. But it shows Layla Ramsey making the withdrawal. She wore a wig to hide her blonde hair, but I caught her putting it on by the ATM camera outside the bank."

"Wow, that's impressive," Diana told him with a smile.

Sam shifted in his seat. It was actually nice seeing a cop be this thorough. Even one that was clearly not having any qualms about blurring professional and personal lines.

"Thank you. Just doing my job." Wickham responded with a grin.

"We appreciate it. So, with what we heard from Bailey, we need to look for this cabin. Is it possible to get bank records to see if he used a credit card or something?" Sam interjected, feeling like this was quickly becoming the Diana and Wickham show.

"Actually, we probably already have that information since he was being looked into in relation to Layla's death."

"Good, then we shouldn't have to wait on a warrant," Brent added to the conversation for the first time. Everyone just kind of stared at him. They were recording, and it was a little weird. Because he usually hung back to let them do the show stuff.

The food arrived before the conversation picked up again.

"So, what do you think?" Pete asked Diana.

"This is delicious. You know if you ever come to my neck of the woods. There's a place you'll love. They have a Honey Pecan Chicken entrée that's to die for."

"I'll keep that in mind," Wickham replied with a smile.

Sam had remained mostly quiet to watch everything unfold with their conversation, and it was strange to watch. This was the type of vibe they'd had when he drove her home from the bar, on the plane, and by the pool. But Wickham, not having brought this emotional chaos into her life, wasn't being held back by guilt, like he was. Sam knew he had to find a way to fix their relationship.

Honesty was a core value of his, and if he was being honest with himself. This case was no longer about telling Reagan's story; it was about helping Diana find closure.

"So what happens next for you guys?" Pete asked after a few moments of eating their food.

"Well. I think we want to find where that road trip video was filmed. Everything is pointing us up north, so I figure we'll pack up and head north on the I-5 and wait for you to give us more information about his credit card transactions." Sam said.

"That kinda sounds like a wild goose chase," Diana commented. Her face had an introspective look on it, like she was racking her brain about how to do this in an easier way.

It was fascinating to Sam to watch her wheels turning like this.

"No, we can save time by analyzing the film for more landmarks. We didn't even look that closely at it before. And with really useful things like Google Maps Street View, I bet we can narrow it down." She suggested.

"She's not wrong." DeMarcus also piped up. Filming had been paused so he could eat.

Or maybe it was still going. Sam wasn't sure DeMarcus's phone was being held up at an angle by his water glass. The kid didn't know when to quit. He thought with pride at how well he was growing into a true professional.

He had met DeMarcus and his family when his brother, Jayden, had been killed. They had become his favorite neighbors. So when he got into videography in high school, it was amazing to watch his talent grow.

And now that they've been working together, they've really become good friends. After an incident on his last case, he realized doing this podcast alone was a recipe for trouble. DeMarcus was a stabilizing presence in his life on the road. Something he hadn't known he needed until he saw him in action with Diana earlier.

"Fine, we'll try to analyze the video more and get it narrowed down, and wait for more information about the boyfriend," Sam said.

"Great! I love it when a plan comes together." Diana said with a smile.

"So tell me about this motorcycle creep," Wickham asked.

"Yeah, he followed us for a good 20 minutes in traffic. Sam here got out to 'Ask him for Directions.' to get the plate for you." Diana told him.

Wickham raised an eyebrow at Sam.

"Then tell him what you did," Sam encouraged her. He didn't bother to hide how upset he still was about that incident.

Diana said nothing.

"I told her to wait in the car, but she didn't listen. That guy could have been anyone we've been poking around, and it seems someone may not like it."

Wickham took a deep breath before turning to Diana.

"Listen, I know I don't know y'all well, but for the love of god, be careful. Even if it's unrelated to this case, some parts of town aren't all that safe. We've seen a rise in carjackings lately. It could have been that. Hell, you've experienced it by getting robbed on your first day here."

Diana tried to interrupt him, but he kept going.

"Situational awareness and not being an idiot will keep you safe for the most part, but don't take chances. Call us, we can help. There's no reason to risk yourself unnecessarily."

Sam felt smug that he was saying basically the same thing he had. But it really wasn't fair. He got Diana's attitude. Wickham got her understanding.

Wickham had a way of putting them all at ease, and they could enjoy the rest of their meal talking about random things from sports to guns, to food. However, when they went to leave for the night, he lingered behind with Diana at the door, and Sam could hear him ask.

"So, what are your plans for the rest of tonight?"

Diana looked at him before turning back to Wickham to say.

"I'm gonna analyze that video and then try to get some sleep." She replied, and he could tell she was stifling a yawn.

"Isn't that what they're for? If you're only in L.A. for a short time, do you want to see any of the sights?" Sam had to give him credit; he was persistent.

"No, I'll have to make another trip for that. Right now, I'm staying focused on the case. It's what Reagan deserved the first time around. I will not let her down again."

Sam could see Wickham's eyes darting between him and Diana, as he had stopped to wait for her.

"Ok. Well, call or text me if you need anything. I'm only one phone call away."

"I appreciate that." She responded, and then she gave him a hug before hurrying up with their group that was walking to the car.

The green-eyed monster once again rose in Sam, but he decided he needed to focus on the positive here. Diana was coming home with him, not Wickham.

Chapter 11

They got back to the house and drifted into separate corners. It was still early, barely 7 p.m.

Sam had work to do.

Diana had taken over reviewing the video footage, giving Sam the space to chase down a lead he didn't want her pursuing. Not until he was sure. Not until he knew who the man in that photo really was. If his gut was right, this guy was a repeat offender, probably already listed somewhere on a registry. But L.A. was massive. Even if he was local, searching the sex offender registry was like digging for a needle in a haystack.

To help narrow it down, he'd looped in Brent and DeMarcus. They were combing through comment sections on Reagan's old videos, flagging anything creepy or obsessive. Then trying to trace who was behind the usernames. Grunt work. Stuff cops get to eventually, once there's time, or a task force. But someone had to do it now.

Still, after a while, Sam's eyes were blurry, and his thoughts kept circling Diana. He needed a break. He needed to make amends.

He knocked on her door.

"Who is it?" she called out.

"It's just me. Can we talk?" He said, waiting behind the closed door.

"Fine. Come in."

He opened the door and stepped inside, and closed it behind him.

She was sitting on the bed with her laptop open, now wearing something just as sexy as her red dress.

A satin purple pajama set clung to every curve. He wasn't sure what he expected her to be wearing just before bed, but maybe he should have.

"How are you holding up?" he asked gruffly, fighting the instinct to move closer to her.

"I'm fine." She replied. Her tone was dismissive, and it snapped him back to reality. She was still mad at him.

"Well, I wanted to come tell you the truth about something."

"Oh really? What is that?" she asked.

"I'm an asshole," he said bluntly.

Diana didn't even look up when she responded.

"I figured that one out for myself."

"No, I mean, like not being 100% forthcoming on all the new evidence we had when we first met. That it was withheld to create more of a splash for the content. And that you were 100% correct to call me out over that."

"It's what anyone in your position..."

He cut her off.

"No, don't make excuses for me. It was the wrong call to make, because you, Diana, are not the bad guy in this."

Maybe he'd said it before. Maybe not. But she needed to hear it now.

Diana looked up at him. He caught the flicker of sadness and guilt flash across her face.

"Are you so sure?" she asked, steady but quiet. "I'm the one who should've pushed for answers sooner, should have seen what must have been happening."

He shook his head. "You had every reason not to. Taking care of your mom, holding your entire world together, it's a miracle you're standing here. And honestly, we never would've gotten this far without you."

Her mouth parted slightly. He could tell she was surprised he said that.

"You really mean that?"

"Of course I do." A wry smile tugged at his lips. "Remember, I'm the truth hunter."

Her breath caught. Their eyes locked.

"But that's not the truth I really wanted to tell you."

"Then what is?" she asked, voice softer now.

"You remind me of the man I used to be. The one who wasn't such an asshole."

Her lips twitched. "I do?"

"Yes, dammit, what I'm trying to say..."

Why was this so hard to say? He thought before saying the thing that had driven him to come find her.

"Is ...I don't just see you as someone related to my podcast. That I care what this investigation is doing to you. And that I notice your pain every time someone mentions Reagan's name. That I understand how hard all of this must be for you. That I'm here if you need a hug or a shoulder to cry on. No cameras, no bullshit, just me."

She didn't say anything for what felt like an eternity.

"I appreciate that. Thank you." He noticed she wasn't exactly meeting his eye when she said that, and he didn't know what that meant.

Maybe she was still mad about their argument earlier. Or still wanted to keep things as professional as possible. But he could tell. One way or another, there were too many sparks between them for this not to end up getting personal feelings involved, and he was done trying to pretend otherwise.

He would wait for the investigation to be completed. But he wanted to make his intentions and his motivations for needing to keep her safe clear.

"Ok, good...have you found anything yet?" He said, suddenly shifting back into professional mode to break the tension that had been building.

He'd finally moved away from the door to get closer to her, his hands clasped behind his back so he could see what she was working on.

"Yes, I took a screenshot of the video and used AI to identify the type of trees seen in the background, which are native to Northern California and Southern Oregon. Then I've just been using Google Maps to figure out what mountain that is. I'm pretty sure it's Mount Shasta." She said, standing up from the bed and handing him the laptop so he could see how the video matched up with the street view.

"Really, that's amazing." He was impressed at how she had come up with a solution to help their investigation.

"Thank you." She didn't look happy, just sad.

After a few moments, she said. "I just keep watching her in this video, and now that I know everything that was going on with her. I just wonder, how many times has she worn that fake smile around us? And we never knew the difference."

Tears had rolled down her cheeks, and Sam couldn't help himself anymore. He set the laptop down on the bed and pulled her into his arms.

She clung to him, and his heart broke for her as she sobbed into his chest.

"Hey...." He drawled out quietly after a few minutes, and she turned to look up at him.

"She didn't want you to know. Can't you see it's obvious? You and her grandmother were her happy place. She didn't want anything to taint that." He said as tears were still welling up in her eyes.

"That's what I see. She didn't want you to know." He started brushing the tears off her cheeks with his thumbs as he touched her face.

His gaze was drawn to her trembling lips. A little voice in his head told him. Not the time, not the time, not the time. While the idea of kissing those tears away entered his head.

So he settled for a forehead kiss instead. And he could feel her relax in his arms and lean into it.

When was the last time she had someone to take care of her? He wondered. When it was clear, she was always so used to taking care of everyone else.

But then her phone rang, and she pulled away. Not looking at him. The emotions of the night must have them both feeling a little raw.

"What the hell is going on?" He could hear Ray yelling from her phone.

"What are you talking about?" She asked him.

"Did they not show you their fucking teaser for your first episode?"

"No, we didn't have time today. Why?"

"Go fucking watch it." He sounded livid.

"Ok, I will. I'll call you back."

"Please do."

She hung up the phone and turned to him.

"What's wrong with the teaser?"

"I'm not sure. Brent said he was going to have it posted at 9 pm. I'm guessing he meant Eastern time zone."

"You haven't seen it either?"

"I was with you all day. I didn't get a chance. So I'm just as confused as you are."

"Well, apparently it's enough to make my friend Ray have a conniption, so I guess we'd better watch it."

She sat back down on the bed and used the laptop to pull up his website. He moved to where he could look over her shoulder.

The video started with Sam outside her house.

"We are here in front of the house of Reagan Ramsey's last living relative, Her Aunt, Diana Ramsey. To find out why she hasn't tried to get answers in any of the five years since her niece disappeared?"

Diana glared at him, but they kept watching. He had a sinking feeling in his chest. They had never re-filmed the intro after realizing the premise was all wrong.

Then it started with the phone call they had recorded asking if they could interview her, and his blood ran cold.

"We are doing a story about your niece, Reagan Ramsey. Have you had any contact with her since she went missing 5 years ago?"

"Seriously?"

"Listen. I want to interview you, if that's okay. I want to go back and reopen Reagan's case with fresh eyes, because I want to find her and bring her home."

"Whatever dude, so how do you want to do this?"

"I can meet you at your house tomorrow, around 4 pm. It'll be me, my producer, and our camera guy. I'll need something like a kitchen table to lay the evidence out on. Other than that, it'll be just a normal conversation with me. The goal is to go over what we thought we knew and what we know now."

"Not really my thing,"

Let me show you my findings; then we can conduct the interview and begin working on her cold case.

"Yeah, profiting off other people's misery sounds tricky. Okay. Show me what you got, and then I'll decide if I want to do an interview."

She threw the laptop across the room. Luckily, years of playing sports gave him great reflexes, and he caught it.

"YOU MOTHERFUCKER! GET OUT OF MY ROOM!" She was yelling at the top of her lungs.

"No. Listen to me, I did not approve of this!" Sam was furious at himself for not reviewing it before it was posted. The dishonesty in her clips being reworked and edited to make her seem callous and motivated by money had him ready to wring Brent's neck.

She threw a pillow next. It landed a few feet away.

"I DON'T BELIEVE YOU! GET OUT!" She was about to kick his ass. The pre-threat indicators were all there. Eyes flashing, pulse visibly racing, her face turning ruddy with rage.

She shoved him toward the door, palms hitting his chest.

Sam caught her wrists, gently at first, then firmer as she twisted. He maneuvered her arms behind her back, careful not to hurt her, but stopping her from escalating things into something they'd both regret. Suddenly, they were flush. Chest to chest.

She was furious. Justifiably so.

But as he looked down into her eyes, his pleaded with hers. He needed her to believe him.

"Diana, please. Just listen. I. Didn't. Do. This."

Her breathing was ragged. Her pulse kicked at her throat. But her resistance softened. His voice, low, earnest, was cutting through the rage.

"It's my fault. I should've reviewed it. But I didn't approve of it. I swear, Diana. I would never do that to you."

Just then, the door behind him crashed open, and DeMarcus and Brent were there. Shock on their faces.

"What's going on? Sam, what are you doing in here?" DeMarcus asked, confused, taking in her pajamas and his proximity to the bed, and how they were standing.

"No, it's not what it looks like. Brent, what the hell were you thinking?" He said, releasing her and turning on Brent.

"Did you watch the whole teaser?" He asked cautiously, taking a few steps back with his hands up.

"No, we didn't get that far! How could you!" He yelled at Brent. The buddy who recommended him was going to get a very nasty email. The incompetence could no longer be ignored.

"You're fired. I will book you a flight home tonight, but you are no longer welcome; get out."

And he physically removed Brent from her bedroom. DeMarcus lingered, and Sam heard him say to Diana.

"I have no idea what's going on... But I'm on your side."

****

Diana stood frozen in the center of the room. Her chest heaving, her hands still curled into fists. The silence in the wake of his retreat felt deafening.

DeMarcus had closed the door behind him. She moved towards it. Rage, pain, and confusion all coursing through her. She leaned her head against the panels. Trying to sort through everything she was feeling.

Rage that Sam, the guy so hung up on honesty, had edited her words out of context to fit a narrative.

Pain that for a moment she had dropped her walls, and he'd seen her vulnerable as the guilt and worry over Reagan had made her emotional.

Confusion at the fact that he hadn't tried to defend himself with how the teaser made her look. He'd been angry too... at Brent.

She needed answers.

She took a deep, calming breath, then headed back to where her phone was and called Ray back.

"Did you watch the whole thing?" He asked, his tone a lot calmer than it had been on his first call.

"No. Sam was in here. We were having a moment of a sort, when you called and we watched the butchered phone call and I threw him out."

"Well, you should have kept watching," Ray said. The irritation was not completely out of his tone.

"Why...?"

"Well, right at the end of the butchered phone call, they did a little record scratch sound effect and then said something along the lines of Diana Ramsey was a surprise. From the outside of this case, one would assume she didn't care, but that is not what we found when we talked to her. They then played the actual call and said it was clear you do care about your niece. But lies have tainted what you thought you knew. And now you've joined forces to venture to California to find out what really happened to Reagan Ramsey." He finished quoting the last line.

"Oh...well, I still don't like it," Diana whispered. The rage she felt started to die down. She didn't know how he had done it in the moment. Most men would have run when she got that angry. But the fact that he stayed, didn't back down, cast blame, or make excuses, did more for calming her down than anything else.

"Please tell me you didn't commit a murder over this," Ray said, half joking, half serious. He knew her well.

She giggled.

"No.. not yet. Day ain't over either." She could hear his eyes rolling.

"Traci wants the phone. I have you on speaker, and she wants to find out more about this 'moment' you mentioned."

"Hi Traci. How are you and the kids?" Diana said, trying to delay the inevitable questions she wasn't ready to answer.

"How are you?" Damn, it was good to hear her voice. Hearing it made her long to head back home, where things were simpler and less painful than being here with these strangers. Never knowing what the next clue would uncover.

"A little less homicidal than I was 5 minutes ago."

"That's good. You mentioned a moment ago. What happened?"

"Nothing much, just me crying, and he gave me a hug."

"A hug...?"

"Yeah..it was a very good hug..."

"Why were you crying, hon?"

Diana paused. It was hard for her to burden her friend with the chaotic emotions she was feeling.

"I feel like I barely knew my own niece." She said with a heavy sigh. "She had all this shit going on and I thought we were pretty close, given the distance, and she never said a goddamn word about any of it."

"She didn't want to spoil the time she had with you guys."

"That's what he said."

"Sounds like he's not a horrible person."

"Sometimes he is. He got jealous because I flirted with the cop this morning to help get us answers."

"Really!"

"I was chalking it up to professional jealousy, but he said something tonight that made me think it was something else."

"What was that?"

"Essentially, that he cares..." And Diana couldn't help but bask in the memory of that moment. It was probably the nicest, kindest thing he could have said. It reminded her of how things were between them before they arrived in L.A.

But pride kept her mouth shut. So she watched him stand there nervously at the door, waiting for a response she wasn't ready to give yet.

"AWWW."

And then Traci giggled for a moment.

"And how do you feel?" She asked.

Of course, she'd ask that. But it was impossible to discern anything she may or may not be feeling about him from this overwhelming drive to find answers about Reagan.

"I don't know? Right now, everything is about Reagan. I need to find her. The more I find out about what is going on, the more scared for her I become."

"You're dodging the question. Do you like the man?" Traci pushed back.

"I mean, yes, he's nice to look at, and he laughs at my jokes. I know he values honesty, and after my last relationship, that's a nice change. But he lives in DC and..."

"Baby steps, you're already thinking of steps 20-25. You need to find out if you even like him like that before you think about logistics."

"You're right."

"But if you're already thinking about steps 20-25, it kind of sounds like you do."

"Maybe...I don't know. Maybe if I can go more than 5 hours without throwing things at him, I could find out."

"You threw things at him?" Traci said with a strangled yell.

"Yes, although technically one was a pillow, so it barely counts," Diana said as she picked up the pillows and the laptop from the ground where she'd thrown them.

"What did you throw that wasn't a pillow?"

"My laptop." She said a little sheepishly. There wasn't a crack in the screen, but she's pretty sure there had been a little plastic piece on that corner previously.

"Jesus. Well, yeah, let's make that a rule, can he go at least 6 hrs without pissing you off? That seems like a reasonable standard to have."

Diana giggled.

"I love you, Traci. I'm so glad you're my best friend."

"I love you, too, kiddo. And you know we're all praying you find Reagan and that she's ok."

"I know. I'll keep you guys posted. But I'm gonna go see how much my temper is gonna cost me on a new laptop. I'll talk to you guys tomorrow. The plan is to head north and see if we can't find more evidence about her last movements. We'll be up near Mount Shasta."

"Sounds beautiful. I'll talk to you next time."

Brent was about to lose his job because of her reaction; she needed to do something.

She got up and put the matching robe on to her satin pajama set and marched into the kitchen, where Sam was on the phone.

"I need to talk to you."

"I'll call back in a moment." He said and hung up.

"Listen, I am so sorry. I had no idea what Brent was going to do. I thought we were all on the same page about how to showcase this story." He started. His eyes were earnest with apology.

Diana held a hand up. He stopped. He looked so forlorn. Maybe he really did care, and this spark meant something to him.

"Brent could have done it a lot differently, but we didn't give him a chance and watch the whole thing."

He looked surprised.

"If you're willing to give him the benefit of the doubt, so am I," Sam said cautiously.

"Let's go see if we owe him an apology." She took a deep breath, and they headed up the stairs. She wasn't sure which room was Brent's and gave Sam a confused look before he pointed at the door in front of them to the right.

She knocked softly.

"Brent, I want to talk to you."

He opened the door, and she felt a sharp pang at his red-rimmed eyes.

"My friend who called me and told me I needed to watch the whole thing, so I figured we should do that together."

"Yes, yes, then you'll see what I tried to do." He said excitedly as he waved them inside the room where he had taken over a desk meant for a kid, with his computer setup.

DeMarcus also ventured in, and they waited with bated breath.

The part Ray had described went a lot harder emotionally than he had let on. And it really proved the narrative that she was all in on this quest to find Reagan. They also went over the outline of the first episode, which included video from the police station where she took down the attempted robber, the emotional meeting with Bailey, and the dinner with Sergeant Wickham. It had her looking like a Valkyrie on a mission.

She hugged Brent from behind his chair and gave him a kiss on the top of his bald head.

"Thank you, Brent. This is lovely." She told him.

"We're all on your side, kid. We want you to find Reagan and to bring her home." He said in a fatherly way.

He was the oldest of the crew, and Diana realized she didn't know him well, but considering losing this job potentially had him crying his eyes out as a grown 50-something-year-old man, told her this job meant a lot to him.

"Unfire him, Sam," Diana said, turning around.

"Who runs this ship?" He asked with a smirk he was trying to suppress.

"I do. Naturally, I've led a mutiny." She retorted. Putting her hands on her hips. While he smiled down at her.

He took a deep breath and said,

"Brent, I apologize for losing my temper. We would, as the lady says, love to have you stay on this project. Just run everything by us before you release it."

"Sure thing, boss," Brent replied with a smile.

"Now that we're all on the same page, Brent and I were talking, are we sure going north is the right move, not doing more interviews here?" DeMarcus asked.

"We can always come back, I just think we need to trace her last movements and that may help us know what questions to ask if we don't find anything," Diana said.

They all nodded.

DeMarcus went back to his room, and Diana followed Sam downstairs. The house had a bar in the outdoor kitchen that was fully stocked. He made a beeline for it. Diana followed.

She took a seat on the barstool, and he went behind the bar to grab each of them a beer.

"Do you ever stop to wonder why are we the way we are?" She asked him.

"Not really," he said, looking for the bottle opener before deciding to just use the edge of the countertop.

"I'm sorry for throwing things; that was childish." She said before taking a sip. She hated beer, but the day called for some type of alcohol, for sure.

"The way this investigation has been going, it won't be the last time. But don't worry, I have good reflexes."

She grinned at him.

"Seriously, though, if you can forgive me for that idiotic comment from the police station, I can get past some airborne objects, and let's say we just start over with a clean slate."

Diana nodded.

He took the stool next to her, and they both turned to look out over the pool that was reflecting the moonlight.

"What's Brent's story?"

Sam raised an eyebrow at her. It looked like he was waiting for her to say something, and that wasn't what he expected.

"One of my sponsors recommended him. I'd gotten to be good friends with the rep there, and he is their uncle. I know his wife just left him for another man and took his kids. And he'd just about bankrupted himself in lawyer fees just to get visitation rights."

"Wow, I'm so sorry."

"Yeah, it happens."

"Like it happened to you?" Diana asked. Curious about the man behind the professional podcaster persona, he usually showed her.

"In her defense. I was gone a lot, and I had a lot to learn about how to be a good husband. And I'm sure you can tell. Sometimes I'm a slow learner. I was oblivious to a lot of the issues."

"I've never understood that. Like if we were dating, and for whatever reason, I wasn't happy with you. I'd tell you, so you could fix yourself. And if you didn't, then we'd break up. There is no reason to try and ride two horses with one ass."

He choked on his beer with that last comment.

"You never heard that one before, huh?" She said, clapping him on his back to help clear his airway. She waited for him to take another sip.

"It's the same kind of saying as shit or get off the pot. You're holding up the line."

Beer shot out of his mouth as he started shaking with laughter.

"Jesus. Where do you get all of these one-liners?"

"Walmart.. I don't know." She said with a shrug and a grin.

"How are you still single?" Sam asked bluntly.

Diana was surprised he asked that. She hesitated before answering. He valued the truth... time to see if that scared him off.

"Well, there's a meme floating around on the internet of a guy asking. "Girl, what does that mouth do?" Hurt your feelings, probably.".. Yeah, that's me."

"Nah.. I don't believe it." He said, shaking his head.

"I was literally just throwing things at your head." She pointed out matter-of-factly. "Most men would call that a clue, that I should come with a warning label."

"If that was thrown at my head, you have terrible aim. Thrown near my head is more accurate. But it's fine. And I hope you've learned. I'm not most men." His grin was infectious, and he was starting to do that thing again with his eyes that were making her feel a lot warmer than the beer was.

"I don't know. I work a lot, and taking care of my mom took up a lot of my time. I also quickly become a creepy girlfriend who enjoys talking about marriage and babies way too soon. What's the term? Stage 5 clinger?"

"Work, and your mom, I see, could cramp your style, but no, you don't give off stage 5 clinger vibes. What's the real reason?"

"I honestly don't know. The guys I've dated before were nice, but we'd always end up better off as friends than as a couple."

He smiled at her, and she just noticed how they were sitting. Leaning back against the bar, his arm stretched out behind her. Not touching, but his body language was definitely saying things.

"But what about you? Have you dated since your divorce?"

He took another sip of beer.

"A little, but like you, I work and travel a lot."

"I bet you have so many airline miles."

He chuckled.

"Yeah...with every airline known to man."

She watched the beer bottle go to his mouth and his strong throat take the last few gulps as he drained it.

His black hair was ruffled, his chiseled jawline shown to advantage in the side profile she had of him now.

"You typically work out a lot, don't you?" She said, changing the subject.

He turned and looked at her again, surprised.

She could tell her robe had come undone somewhat as his gaze couldn't help but travel down, and she felt heat start to crest her cheeks.

"Yeah, it's about the only hobby I can do while I travel so much. Every hotel pretty much has a gym, or I keep a membership with a couple of the national brands. So I usually get up around 5 and go do that every other day."

"Well, one hobby I would like to do while we are here is going to a range."

"Really, a gun range?"

"Yeah, I've got a feeling between the creepy biker, the car with the flat tire, a little too conveniently blocking us in, and that robber who attacked me today...it won't be the only thing we face as we find out more of the shady shit going on. I can't have a gun here because of California and its stupid laws, but I'm sure I can get some pepper spray or a taser or something. Gun ranges usually carry that type of stuff."

"Sure, we can do that before we head to Mount Shasta. But you know if having a gun makes you feel safer...I know some people." He said with a serious look on his face.

"...what kind of people? People who will sell me a gun and not go through the proper government paperwork?"

"For you, I'd be willing to make a few phone calls if that made you feel safer while you were here...or I can hire security."

"Oh, that is so sweet. I think we'll be fine," she said, patting him on the arm and letting it linger there. His hand briefly went to where her hand was and gave it a squeeze.

"I just don't like breaking laws or relying on others for my personal safety. If things get really sideways, we'll call the cops. Reagan would be the first person to not want me to put myself in danger to find her. I mean, that's what this investigation is really about, helping the cops have enough information to find her. Right?"

He reached up to tuck a strand of hair behind her ear.

Diana froze in the moment, watching him take the strand and rub it between his fingers for a moment before releasing it.

Her heart was beating in double time.

He took a deep breath, and she looked at the stern line of his lips, anticipating him to lean in and kiss her.

But he took a deep breath and looked away. Breaking eye contact.

"We should get to bed. I know it's technically still early here, but I think my biological clock is still set to Eastern time."

"You're right," Diana said, standing up with him.

"Tomorrow is likely going to be just as heart-wrenching and emotional as today. Just know I'm here every step of the way with you."

"I know. And I appreciate it. Patting him on the shoulder, she said, before turning to go inside and towards her room. These little moments were adding up to something. If she was asked again how she felt, she had a clearer answer now.

It was no longer just wishing they'd met under different circumstances. It was starting to feel like it had the potential to be something a lot more than that.

"Good night, Diana." He said before heading up the stairs.

"Good night, Sam." She said, closing the door to her room.

Chapter 12

The next morning for breakfast, Sam made pancakes, and they were actually good. He even went to the trouble of adding blueberries, which were Diana's favorite. Nothing like eating carbs and telling yourself it's healthy because it included fruit. Just like pickles on cheeseburgers made them healthier.

Brent shared with them the response they'd gotten to the teaser.

"The teaser post has gone viral. Over 4 million interactions since I posted it last night. Also, I'm starting to get phone calls from news outlets asking about our investigation and if Diana would be willing to do an interview."

"You've got to be kidding me!" Diana groaned. This was bad, I mean it was good, it may generate fresh interest and new leads to help their investigation. But Diana had no desire to be in the public spotlight.

"So much for your peaceful life," Brent joked. Sam raised an eyebrow at him. "This will die down eventually. We've seen this before with the Kendrick Johnson case I covered for the Post. Lots of interest originally, but died out after a few weeks." Sam said, eating a piece of bacon.

"God, I hope so. I can only act like a normal human for so long before eventually I will say something that will offend someone or lose my temper. Or you know, just be weird in general." Diana said, before taking another bite of her pancakes.

"Maybe I'll just talk about guns all the time and they'll cancel me immediately, and that way it won't be such a surprise that I'm not mainstream media material."

"You'll be fine," Sam assured her.

"Let's just get this show on the road and find Reagan. I feel like we're lollygagging." Diana told them, standing up from the table to take her plate to the sink.

"Yes, ma'am," Sam said, following her.

They went to load up the Tahoe and noticed a tire was flat.

The delay was annoying. The anticipation to get on the road was making her feel antsy she paced as they worked to get it changed.

Once the tire was replaced, they quickly loaded up the Tahoe and headed out.

"Oh, I just remembered. We'd talked about stopping at a gun store to pick up some pepper spray and stuff. Can we do that real quick?"

"Sure," Sam said, updating his GPS.

They pulled into the parking lot of Evan's Gun World and walked inside. It was a beautiful building with all black glass.

Diana noticed the others walking around in awe. Have they never been to a gun range before? she wondered. Except Sam, who was clearly interested in some items behind the glass case.

She was able to find a couple of good defensive options. She wasn't a fan of pepper spray. There was always the feeling that with her luck. She would always end up downwind if she tried to use it.

But a tactical pen, a couple of knives would help.

It would be really nice to have a ranged weapon, because letting people get too close to you can be a recipe for disaster.

However, because she could not legally carry a firearm, her options were limited to a Taser with projectile probes or a pepper ball launcher.

"Sam, which of these would you choose?" She asked, looking at them. Neither was cheap, and she had little experience with either, so maybe carrying one wouldn't be a smart choice without training, but she felt like they needed something.

Thank God for YouTube. She would watch some training videos on the road trip. It wasn't as good as in-person training, but it would work in a pinch.

"Get both."

"What? Really?" She was shocked. That would put this little shopping trip over $1000, which was a crazy amount of money to spend on not even a gun.

"Anything to make you feel safer, and honestly, I didn't personally enjoy having to watch you go hands-on with that homeless guy with the knife."

"He was like 5'5 and 100 lbs. soaking wet. It barely counts. Plus, I think he wanted to go to jail because he was hungry."

"He counts, so do the creepy biker and all the other weird shit going on," Sam said, moving closer.

His mouth firmed, and he looked again at the Taser and the launcher, and said. "Actually, we should all be taking our self-defense more seriously. We should get a few options to choose from. Go crazy. Outfit the whole team."

Diana stared at him.

"Are you sure you want me to do that, because I can spend some serious money in a place like this?" she warned him.

It was like a dream come true having a guy take her to a gun store and say, 'Get whatever you want.' But she didn't like men to spend money on her. It made her feel weird. She didn't want Sam to think she was the kind of woman who was impressed by money. She wasn't.

"I'm serious. Whatever you recommend." He said, waving the others over so they could look over the options.

"Well, in that case, we'll get two of each of these, and then everyone gets two knives, a tactical pen, and two flashlights."

"Why two of everything?" DeMarcus asked.

"Well, there's a saying that two is 1 and 1 is none. If someone were to disarm me like I did that homeless guy, then I'm at their mercy. If I had a backup. I still have options. Options mean survival."

"Makes sense to me. Go for it." Sam nodded.

"Do y'all know how to use any of this?" Diana asked as they moved to the checkout line.

"Not much," Brent said.

"Yeah, pretty much only what I've seen in movies," DeMarcus added.

Sam raised a brow. "Like you, I know more about guns than I do this stuff, but I have been pepper-sprayed and tased before. For an article."

"Okay," Diana said, taking mental stock of the group.

"None of this is magic. In California, we've got to follow the rules. No pepper rounds in the launcher, for example. But impact rounds still hurt like hell, and that's usually enough to make someone rethink their life choices."

She looked at each of them.

"This stuff is about buying time. Getting space. It's not meant to stop a fight so much as let you escape one."

She paused. "The best defense is not needing it. But if it comes to that? I want all of us walking out in one piece."

"That'll be $4,957.63," The cashier told her as she checked out. Diana blanched at the total. That was an insane amount of money. Even in California, where everything was more expensive.

"Are you still sure?" She asked as Sam handed over his credit card.

"Why do you keep asking that?"

"I've never had a guy spend money on me like this. It's not what I'm used to."

That was a lot of money for anyone. Especially someone she had only really just met. Part of her brain was trying to remind her of that fact. Yet she already felt more comfortable around him than she had with anyone else in years.

"Don't worry, this is a business expense. But even if it wasn't, I would still want you to feel safe."

And she stood there looking up at him. Their gazes locked. And his words from the night before, that he cared about what she was going through, echoed in her mind.

Just then, her phone rang. It was Sergeant Wickham.

"Hello?"

"Hey Diana, I wanted to let you know I was able to track down the cabin rental. It was in Ashland, Oregon, just over the border. If you get on I-5 North. It'll take you right there."

"That's amazing, thank you. We'll head there now. We'll check in with the local cops when we get there and have them go with us to the property and see if we can't find any evidence."

"Yes, please do, I can't really do too much till Detective Diaz is freed up from her homicide trial on looking into this officially, and it's not really procedure to let civilians do too much in an investigation where it could turn dangerous. Let alone a chain of custody or fruit of the poisonous tree issue. But I'm smart enough to know it'll be easier to work with you than against you."

Diana smiled into the phone.

"I appreciate your thorough understanding of the situation."

"Well, I will admit I had help. Your friend Ray Jordan called and ran me through the riot act to keep you safe and gave me a warning about what I was getting into." He said with a chuckle.

"Oh, he did?" Diana wasn't surprised.

"Just keep me posted if you find anything. I'll reach out to the police up there and get you a point of contact and text you the address of the cabin."

"Thank you so much, Pete. I promise to keep you posted." She hung up.

"So we have an address?" Sam asked her.

"Yep, but we're gonna talk to the local cops first, so let's get on the road. How long is it gonna take to get to Ashland?"

"Like 11-12 hrs. Why?"

"Jesus... I think we should get another rental. This is gonna get cramped for everyone being on the road that long."

"I agree. DeMarcus, set up some stationary cameras in here with me and Diana, and you and Brent ride in the other vehicle."

She barely made it to the parking lot before an angry text message from Ray arrived.

You forgot to mention you almost got robbed!

She texted back.

Key word...almost.

She was not looking forward to that conversation the next time she talked to Ray and Traci. Pete must have told him. Fucking blabber mouth.

She texted Pete.

You just had to say something to Ray about the incident in front of the police station. Geez, thanks.

He texted back

You're welcome

Diana rolled her eyes.

They made a quick stop at a Hertz outlet, where DeMarcus and Brent transferred to a pickup truck with four-wheel drive. Heading into the mountains, they wanted to be prepared for anything.

Once they were alone, driving north, Diana couldn't stop staring at the stationary camera pointed at her face.

She turned toward the window, trying to focus on the scenery as the city fell away behind them. The thick, industrial smog, which had been the first thing she'd noticed getting off the plane, began to lift as they reached the quieter stretches of rural California. The air smelled cleaner now.

Still, she couldn't shake the feeling of being in a fishbowl.

It was strange and stifling, making her reluctant to say anything at all. Her phone buzzed again. Then again. Her social media was blowing up, as friends, acquaintances, even strangers reacting as they realized she was the woman featured on that podcast. That her niece was the Reagan Ramsey.

She sank into the corner of the passenger seat, scrolling through the comments. Feeling smaller and smaller as people said twisted, hurtful things. About her, about her niece, about the whole show, and their situation. How she must be fucking Sam to get him to invite her to join their investigation.

Sam looked over.

"What are you doing?"

".... nothing."

"It doesn't look like nothing. You look upset."

Diana heaved a gigantic sigh.

"I'm just reading some of the comments."

Sam groaned.

"Never do that. It'll steal your confidence."

"I can see that, but I was curious. After Brent said we had so many views and all my friends, coworkers, and even my neighbor all texted me today, I wanted to see what else was being said."

"You'll drive yourself crazy if you listen to internet trolls. The only thing that matters is finding Reagan. Who cares what random people on the internet say about how you do that?"

That told her he already knew what some comments were saying.

"I suppose, but the audacity of some of these people? It's shocking. But some of them look like clues, like this one saying they've seen her in Mexico last year. Maybe we should read these. What if that's a real clue?"

"That's why we do our investigation and start at the beginning. If we find other tangible evidence that she's in Mexico, then we'll go and re-examine that. But we can't let random people on the internet who have no consequence of being wrong influence how we spend our time and resources."

"You're right, of course, but dang, this is overwhelming," Diana said. But then a news article caught her eye.

"SAM BENSON JUST HAS TO BE A PART OF THE STORY." She read aloud to him.

His head whipped around at her.

She skimmed over the article. It brought up a news story she remembered seeing during his MMIW case about him getting arrested, but she didn't hear this version of events in that article.

During his investigation into the Missing and Murdered Indigenous Women in Nome, Alaska, Benson was arrested for Aggravated Assault. The charges were later dismissed, but evidence shows that a lawsuit and settlement were also covered up.

With his new case, inviting the aunt of the Missing Reagan Ramsey into the investigation is unheard of in professional journalism. Does it show he never learned his lesson about getting involved in a story? Because speculation is running rampant in the comment section, that he may be getting involved with the aunt.

"Who wrote this trash?" She asked him.

"I'm guessing it's my ex-wife, Beth Benson?" He said casually. His hands were gripping the steering wheel.

"How do you know?" Diana was shocked.

"She always likes to ask questions in her articles. It's weird and lazy journalism."

"This bitch..." Diana mumbled to herself as she read the comments on the article basically bashing Sam.

"What happened in Nome? From what I read before, you protected some women. The arrest was just a part of the procedure because the witnesses weren't talking."

Sam looked away and was very quiet. To the point, she wasn't sure he was going to answer her.

"I had wanted to do a story on that subject for years. To help bring more attention to the problem. When I finally got the chance to do the cases I wanted to report on. I knew that one had to be first."

Diana remained silent to let him continue.

"We traveled to 5 different states and a couple of Canadian provinces as well. But Nome, Alaska, was the last stop before tying up the last episode. There was a bar on the edge of town, and several women had gone missing from it, so we went to check it out. I wasn't even going to interview anyone there, just get some B-roll and mention it as one of many places that has this issue. "

Diana got the impression this wasn't easy for him to talk about.

"While there. I noticed a guy being creepy to some girls. I was filming it because I knew it would be great to drive home the point for the last episode. But then he got handsy, and everyone was just watching it happen. Including me at first. Then the man backhanded her across the face, and I'd seen enough."

"What did you do?" She asked.

He stared forward at the road. But she could tell he wasn't really seeing it. But his jaw firmed, and he said in a low, rough voice, dripping with emotion.

"The only thing I didn't do was kill him. His injuries were severe..." He took a deep breath. "Broken jaw, broken ribs, collarbone, hands, and a concussion."

Diana's jaw dropped.

"He was in the ICU for like 3 weeks. The concussion had caused a seizure. "

"Holy shit. What about you? Were you ok? I mean, I know you're ok, you're alive and here, but damn dude." She asked.

She was impressed once again at his unapologetic accountability. He didn't try to sugarcoat, nor hide from exactly what happened.

"He never laid a hand on me, actually. When I got up to confront him, he went for a knife, so once that got found out, I was released."

Diana took a moment to digest that. He wasn't proud of that fight; he wasn't ashamed either.

"Ahh, so we're both 1 and 0 on douchebags with knives, go us!" she said, trying to break the tension.

She watched the mirth rumble in his chest as he fought to keep it in, because this was obviously not a good time to crack jokes. Which, of course, was exactly the time her brain thought of them.

She had always been like that. Ever since her dad got sick and her brother died, being able to cheer her mom up in the darkest of days had become her coping mechanism.

"And this lawsuit? What happened there?" She thought to ask.

"He found out that happened the same day as my divorce got finalized, and was using that to say I was looking for a fight. The prosecutor had refused to charge me, so he tried to sue me for $5 million dollars."

"Are you fucking serious?" Diana was shocked.

"It actually happens more than you think, but luckily I have an insurance thing that was able to get it settled for $200,000, and I didn't have to pay him anything."

"Jesus Christ. That's crazy, Diana said, looking back at her phone.

Realizing she was still pissed at how the article was alluding to Sam being unprofessional, when he'd been nothing but a gentleman, had her brain swirling.

Last night, she'd told Traci he was just a hot guy, but she was keeping her distance because she needed to focus on finding Reagan. However, after everything that had happened and everything she'd learned about him, she realized. He wasn't just a hot guy. He had character and drive, and she admitted to herself. She was starting to catch feelings for him.

But, damn if the timing couldn't have been worse. She looked back at the news story one last time, where they had a picture of Reagan, and there were a lot of emotions, but she decided the petty revenge one was the most productive...and safest one to concentrate on for the moment.

"Ok...hey Sam, can I borrow your phone?"

"Why?" He asked with a raised eyebrow.

"I want to talk to DeMarcus's mom about taxes."

"Taxes..." He said, not believing her for a second.

"Yep..."

"I really don't believe you, Diana. You're actually a terrible liar." He said with a smile.

"Then what do you believe? That I'm gonna tell her what this bitch did, and see if she happens to know her address where I can mail a glitter bomb, or maybe one of those rude Singing Telegrams...I've got a few more ideas, but these are the legal ones." She pouted.

A reluctant smile spread across his face, and there was heat in his eyes as he glanced at her.

"Singing Telegram...what on earth?"

"Listen, I know you probably think it's best just to ignore her and let her try to ride your coattails as you go and do great things, but lucky for you, I'm not you. She needs to be taught a lesson."

"No mailing her things, no spending money to harass her." He said in the sternest of voices he could muster when he was trying not to laugh.

"Ugh...fine, but seriously, dude. You're too nice. You can't just let women like her walk all over you."

"Note taken," he said, voice low. "But lately... there's only one woman I'd let walk all over me."

Oh my god! Does he have a girlfriend?

Wait... no, he said he was single.

The thoughts scrambled through Diana's head, and she must've shown it on her face, because Sam reached over, took her hand, and brought it to his lips, pressing a kiss to the back of it.

Her eyes widened. She glanced pointedly at the cameras, then back at Sam. There was still heat in his gaze, along with a calm certainty that spoke volumes neither of them could say aloud yet.

She took a beat, then finally said, "One day, when this is all over, you and me... we're gonna have to talk. Over drinks. A lot of drinks. But today, sadly, is not that day."

He smiled, slow and sure. Clearly, it was exactly what he'd been hoping to hear.

And Diana's heart soared at the thought he'd wait. He was waiting. And this was no longer just about a podcast case between them.

"Why don't you lean the seat back and take a nap?" Sam said as she yawned.

She didn't argue. Sleep had been hard the past few nights, a strange bed, too many thoughts. But not for the first time, she noticed being in his company made her feel relaxed enough to take a nap.

He woke her up for food about halfway there, and they did a mini interview to talk about what they knew so far, and she got a chance to share more about who Reagan was as a person.

Sam was once again nice, but professional, and not letting her skip the hardball questions. But he also held her hand for a moment and opened the door for her to get back into the vehicle.

When they arrived in Ashland later that night, it was pushing midnight. Brent had booked them a stay in the only hotel in town with a room, but when they got to the counter, they realized.

"What do you mean, it's the last room available?" Sam asked the Night clerk.

"Our Family King Duo is the last room. It has bunk beds in one room and a king bed in the living area. It also has a dining room big enough for all four of you."

Sam looked at Diana.

"I need a roll-away then." He told her.

"I'm so sorry, but they're all taken. It's spring break, so you're actually lucky this one was available after a last-minute cancellation."

"I guess I'll sleep in the tub then," Sam grumbled.

"Stop it," Diana said sternly to Sam. Then turned to the clerk to continue, "It's fine. We'll make it work. Thank you so much for your patience." The clerk smiled at her, and Diana took the keys and led the way to the family duo suite.

After they got their luggage inside the room, they were all just staring at the king bed.

There wasn't a sofa in the room, just a small table with 4 chairs and a couple of desks on either side of the TV stand that encased the mini fridge and microwave.

"So y'all want to draw straws for the top bunk?" Diana asked.

DeMarcus gave her a sarcastic "girl, please" look. And then looked at Sam, and then back at her.

"Brent and I already drew straws. Y'all are gonna have to fight for the covers out here. Goodnight!" He said, pushing Brent into the other room and closing the door.

"I can sleep in the tub," Sam said, heading for the bathroom.

"No, you can't. Just don't make this weird. It's not like I have cooties or something. I slept for like 4 hrs in the car up here. You just go get some rest, and I'll just be over here on my laptop until I get tired. By then, I figured you'll probably be getting up early to work out so we won't actually be sleeping together, really." She told him. Getting her laptop out and setting it up on the desk.

"If you're sure. I'm just sorry they said it was the last room."

"Hey, look on the bright side. At least we have a room." She said with a smile,

Sam continued to the bathroom, and Diana could hear the water running as he jumped into the shower.

For someone who was kissing the back of her hand a few hours ago, saying he'd let her walk all over him, he sure was being a prude right now. They were adults...they could control themselves.

But it was interesting seeing this kind of old-school throwback persona emerge from a modern man. But maybe he was right. The lines between professional and personal were getting pretty blurry, and he didn't want to push her too fast. Something she appreciated. But if he could stop treating her like she was made of glass, that would be cool, too.

She started up her laptop and continued to go through Reagan's older videos, looking for clues or signs she must have missed about the horrible things that were going on in her life during this time.

She had pulled out her earbuds and put them on so the room would be quiet for him to sleep, so she didn't hear him finish his shower.

Sam had stepped out of the bathroom, towel slung around his neck, gym shorts riding low, tank top clinging to all of his muscles.

Diana was startled and nearly dropped her laptop.

"Hey! You need to put those guns away!"

He raised an eyebrow as he stopped near the desk. "These guns?" he said, flexing with zero shame. It caught her off guard by his easy smile and humor. It completely disarmed her.

His eyes darkened at her reaction, zeroing in like he could hear every thought. He took a step closer. His gaze was back to that hunter look, and she was prey. Frozen. Waiting.

Then, knock knock, the door connecting their rooms creaked open.

"Y'all got a charger?" DeMarcus asked, poking his head in.

Sam backed away, and Diana released a breath she didn't realize she'd been holding. He fished a spare out of his bag and then lay down. The moment had passed. She pretended to still be watching the screen on her laptop.

The light on the nightstand went off, and the room was dark except for the glow of her computer. He didn't say a word. Neither did she. Both of them knowing it could set a spark neither of them could put out. And as great as it could be, she would feel guilty in the morning for choosing herself over Reagan, even for just a night.

She tried to keep her mind on the video she was watching from when Reagan was 12. But after a while, she couldn't stop her thoughts from wondering what it would be like if she could go join Sam in bed.

She took a deep breath to concentrate again, but it was no use. She took one earbud out and snuck a peek at him in bed. He'd made himself comfortable lying on his side, turned away from her. But he was awake, she could tell by his breathing.

She glanced back at the smiling face of her niece on the screen of the video she'd been watching, and no matter how many times he tried to tell her, it wasn't her fault. She couldn't escape the guilt of not doing more sooner.

Maybe saying no now was her punishment.

She decided to remove herself from the temptation in the bed. And went into the bathroom to take a shower. By the time she returned, he was fully asleep, and she could stop wondering if he was going to say or do something that would move them forward faster.

She felt a yawn coming on. Nighttime showers always made her sleepy. He was still turned away from her towards the far wall. Maybe if she just put some pillows between them and slept on top of the covers, it would be ok. It wouldn't be weird.

Chapter 13

Sam felt the bed sink down under her weight as she climbed into it. He hadn't slept a wink, listening to her move around the room. Listening to the unmistakable sounds of her going to the bathroom, undressing, and getting into the shower.

It was unbelievably hard not to think about her being naked in the next room. The way her eyes had gone hungry washing over him, and her lips had gone soft with a tell-tell hitch in her breathing; had his well-trained instincts wish he'd packed a dozen tank tops.

But her warning about not wanting to do anything until they find Reagan rang in his heart. It wasn't the right time. DeMarcus's timely knock had saved him from letting his instincts take over. But he was quickly realizing, after her adorable reaction to his ex's article, that she was worth waiting for.

He listened to the sounds of her breathing slow and then turn into a steady rhythm as she fell asleep. He was exhausted after the drive and finally willed himself to follow.

When they woke up in the morning, He found her snuggled up to his side, using his arm as a pillow. He looked down at her face. Covered in freckles. Like this, she was the most beautiful woman he'd ever seen. Serene, peaceful. Almost angelic.

He said almost because she chose that moment to roll over, and her fist collided with his nose.

Startled, green eyes opened on her face as he wrenched himself away from the danger.

"What the hell, man?" She yelped.

"I'm sorry you just punched me in the face in your sleep."

"Why was your face near my side of the bed?"

He didn't want to answer that. His physical desire for her was not deterred by the pain in his face one bit.

"I thought you were staying up?"

"I got tired.... wait, are you bleeding?"

"I'm fine." He said, pinching his nose. It didn't feel broken, thank god, but she'd got him good.

He got out of bed and went to the bathroom. It was about 6 am, light not yet coming through the window, but definitely starting to brighten up the sky outside.

When he came back into the room, she had rolled into the middle of the bed and was asleep again.

He got dressed and went to the hotel gym for a workout as part of his routine. It felt good to focus his energy on a productive activity and try not to think about the kind of activity he wished he was taking part in. And then he swung by the continental breakfast to grab food for everyone.

Diana was still asleep; she was now rolled into the blanket like a burrito, and he smiled at the thought. Seeing her unguarded like this made him long to see it more often. He loved her feisty attitude, her intelligence, and her sense of humor, but earning her trust to see behind those walls. That meant more to him than anything.

He heard movement from the guy's room, so he quietly went to the adjoining door and brought them food.

"How's episode one coming along?" He asked Brent.

"I wanna hear how last night was? Get any sleep?" Brent asked with a sly grin on his face. DeMarcus also looked highly interested in his answer.

Sam remained silent. He would say nothing to anyone about anything regarding how he now viewed Diana. Especially before he got this case solved and had some very specific words with her first.

After a few long, drawn-out moments of silence, Brent continued.

"Great, I had DeMarcus do most of the driving yesterday, so I could get it pretty much finished if y'all want to watch it before we head to the police station."

"Sounds good, I'll go wake up sleeping beauty," Sam muttered, turning for the door.

"Diana, time to wake up." He said, sitting on the edge of the bed.

She rolled away from him. He couldn't help but smile.

"Come on, rise and shine." He said tenderly.

She rolled back and opened one eye.

God, he could kiss her right now. The sleepy, befuddled look on her face was adorable.

He held up the muffin and coffee.

"Smart man to bring me food and coffee." She said, sitting up and reaching out for them.

Her hair was deliciously mussed, and he couldn't help but brush it out of her face for her.

She didn't say anything, but he recognized the same look she'd given him last night, and it was getting harder and harder for him to be professional around her.

"Episode one is ready if you want to join us in the other room to watch it." He said.

She nodded.

A few minutes later, muffin and coffee in hand, they crowded around Brent's computer to watch episode one of the podcast.

This covered more of the interview from her house, some highlight shots from the airport, and then everything from their day in L.A. relating to the case. Realizing they had come so far already made Sam proud of how this was shaping up.

Diana really did come off as a bad-ass, like she was wading through the cesspool that is Los Angeles, flipping robbers in karate moves, questioning police, hunting down leads, and showing empathy for Bailey, while pushing for answers.

He felt like he was the sidekick, and she was the hero. A new role for him. But damn, she was impressive.

Watching the video made them eager to get to the local police station and get the lay of the land for this cabin rental.

"Hello, my name is Sam Benson, this is Diana Ramsey, and we were hoping to talk to John Lynch." He said to the receptionist.

However, a voice from an office off the lobby called out. And a tall man in his 60s walked over and shook all of their hands.

"I'm Chief Lynch, how are y'all doing?" He said.

"Good, we were hoping to get some information."

He cut them off.

"Yeah, on Reagan Ramsey, I got a call from your friend at the LAPD. He sent you here on a wild goose chase to get you out of his hair. But, I'll tell you the same thing I told him, ain't never heard of her, seen her, or nothing. He gave me the address of the cabin rental they said was booked. Had the owner check their records, and they said the guests that weekend were a no-show."

"Wickham... did what?" Sam was flabbergasted. He looked at Diana, and her face was frozen in horror at what the Chief was saying.

"Yeah, said something about you guys being followed by someone on a motorcycle. He's afraid that reopening the case is causing a stir, and he wanted you guys away from the action, so to speak."

Diana started shaking. Sam couldn't tell if it was fury or disappointment.

"I'm sorry, honey. I know that's your niece, but whatever you're looking for ain't here." He told them.

Sam put his arm around Diana's shoulders, knowing this must be killing her. Not knowing what to say or to do. He knew he needed to get her out of there.

"Thank you for doing everything you could for us," Sam said, then led Diana back out to the parking lot.

Diana had tears streaming down her face, and she broke free of his grip and stormed down the sidewalk to where there was a community center.

"Give her a moment, guys." He said to Brent and DeMarcus, who looked like they wanted to follow.

She got to a tree, and she punched it, again, and again, and again. Her body was visibly shaking with sobs. He knew she'd been holding a lot of these feelings in this whole time. He told himself to stop. Give her this moment to feel everything she'd been suppressing. When everything inside of him was telling him to go. He had been waiting for this moment to happen since that first episode when she almost threw them out after showing her the picture.

She then fell to her knees, and he couldn't bear it anymore. He walked up behind her and crouched down next to her, and pulled her into his arms. Hoping that when she was ready to listen, he would find the words she needed to hear.

"It's not over. We have more clues we can find. We're not giving up." He told her, his head on top of her hair.

"All this way. A whole 2 days wasted for nothing! Nothing to see, nothing to do, a fucking wild goose chase! And fucking Wickham knew it! What if she didn't have 2 more days? What if she ran out of time before I could get to her? Why didn't I try to find her sooner?" She sobbed, clinging to his shirt.

"Hey, this is not your fault, sweetheart. You didn't know half of what you know now. Please, Diana, don't beat yourself up. You do not deserve to carry this guilt."

"This is so fucked up." She said.

"I know. This whole situation. The lies you were fed by Layla and hell, even Reagan herself. If she had only said something when she had visited you, everything could have been so different."

She moved and looked up at him. Her eyes and nose were red, but still beautiful to him despite the ugly crying.

"You said we had more leads we could follow, like what?"

That's my girl...he couldn't help but think as he watched her take enough deep breaths to calm herself and reorient her focus on the next clue. Damn. She was magnificent.

"That idea you had, about following up with her teacher and the friends she had outside of the business. That was always the backup plan if we didn't find what we needed here."

She was wiping away her tears as more continued to leak out of her eyes. He responded earnestly. Rubbing her arms up and down. She took a deep, shuddering breath.

"So what's next? Do we go back to LA? We know she traveled north. I identified that in her video."

"We can make some phone calls, maybe try to narrow down where to look next. Maybe that Mexico comment you saw will have merit when we talk to someone."

"Ok, let's head back to the hotel and call her school."

He nodded and stood up, and helped her to her feet. His hands went to her waist to steady her. He couldn't resist pulling her in for one more hug and dropping a kiss on top of her head. He had always been a physically affectionate guy. And with her looking like she may break apart again at any moment, he wanted her to know she wasn't alone. Recognizing the loneliness in her drew him like a lodestone as it echoed how lonely he'd been these last few years.

She made him want to be a better version of himself. She had to know his reputation. She'd mentioned looking up his past cases and interviews. Reckless. Immature. Sometimes controversial, even pushing into asshole territory during interviews when he asked the tough questions no one else dared. But for her, he was going to prove he was more than that.

As they returned to the vehicles. DeMarcus and Brent were standing quietly by the passenger side, looking like they wanted to say something. Diana had barely dried her eyes, and Sam's arm was still around her shoulders.

He was checking out the damage she'd done to her hands. They would need to dig out the first aid supplies he always packed with them.

Brent looked at him expectantly.

"No interview just yet. We're heading back to the hotel." Sam told him.

They made the quick drive back to the hotel and were able to secure more rooms that night for everyone to have their own. He and Diana kept the same room they'd been in before, except now he'd move to the bunk bed area.

While Brent and DeMarcus would get adjoining rooms across the hall so they could work on episode two, which will include their wild goose chase and hopefully the promise of new leads after their call to the school.

Chapter 14

Diana set her computer up on the same desk as she had last night. Then looked up the number for Reagan's school. They had taken a moment while unpacking to bandage up her hands, which were badly scraped from punching the tree. And possibly from hitting Sam's nose this morning, but she wasn't going to think about that right now.

It was safer to only be thinking about the next clue.

Sam had been very tender in the ministrations of first aid. And Diana used the time to prepare emotionally for the next step. Because she felt emotionally raw. She was tempted to call Wickham first and yell at him, but in her heart, she knew he was doing what he thought was best.

Sam then approached with the mic pack.

"DeMarcus wants to get every word, so this will help." He said. Clipping the mic to the blue blazer she was wearing today.

"You know I can probably do this myself." She told him.

He paused for a moment, but an interesting smile on his face told her he was thinking of saying something naughty.

She raised an eyebrow at him, waiting for him to have the guts to say whatever it was.

"I know you can, but I doubt you enjoy putting this on you as much as I do."

She had not been expecting that! A nervous chuckle escaped her, and she just had to get him back for that comment.

"Oh, so you're just wanting to cop a feel?"

His fingertips brushed the side of her neck, and he draped the cord over her shoulder and leaned down to whisper in her ear. His warm breath sent goosebumps all down her side.

"Darlin, when this investigation is over and I really get an opportunity to touch you like I want, copping a feel isn't what I plan to do. I will touch, taste, and worship every inch of you. And that, Diana, we'll both enjoy."

Heat flooded her face as she looked up at him in surprise. His wolfish grin said he knew exactly what he was doing. But he moved away, and Brent and DeMarcus arrived so they could get started.

Diana worked to hide how flustered he'd made her, but somehow it also felt like a balm to her tender heart, which just an hour ago felt like it had broken into a million pieces.

She took a deep breath to collect herself. Watching Sam move around the room for last-minute prep. Grabbing a notepad and pen. Then checking the camera angle.

The fact that he'd known exactly what to say to make her feel better was telling her he'd gotten closer than she ever expected. But before she could analyze that feeling too closely, it was time to get started.

She placed the phone call on speaker. Sam pulled up a chair next to her, and DeMarcus gave her the thumbs up from behind the camera.

Reagan had gone to a fancy private school called Belmont.

The phone rang and rang, and eventually someone answered.

"Belmont Preparatory Academy, how may I help you?"

"Hi, my name is Diana Ramsey. My niece Reagan Ramsey went to your..."

"Oh my god, it's Diana Ramsey!" The voice on the other end of the phone squealed so loud Diana recoiled from the phone.

"You're from that podcast Second Look Cases!"

Diana looked up at the guys to see if they were as surprised as she was by the excitement from the lady on the phone. However, the guys were just smiling at her. Like, they knew people were going to basically fan-girl over her.

"Yes, that's right. I'm looking for help to find my niece, Reagan."

"You know, I wondered if you were gonna call. I never thought you actually would, but I thought it might be a possibility. I've only worked here for 3 years, so I didn't know poor Reagan. But I know some of the teachers remember her. They always said she was a nice girl."

"Thank you for saying that. You have no idea how much I appreciate it. Yes, I was hoping to talk to her teacher to see if she knew of anyone she was friends with outside of her work."

"Yes, yes, Miss Linda Jameson was her teacher, and she's still here. Let me get her on the phone for you, sweetie."

"What is your name, if you don't mind me asking?" Diana thought to ask. She was gonna send this woman flowers.

Her positivity and excitement was just the motivation she needed to remind herself that they were still making tons of progress from where they were even a week ago, when she had no clue about any of this.

"Andrea Hopwell, dear. Just hold on for me and I'll be right back."

Hold music played, and Diana awkwardly looked at the guys. She wanted to grab Sam's hand, because it had been so comforting earlier when he held her and acted like he didn't want to let go.

God, it had been years since she felt like she had someone she could turn to when things got crazy. Maybe she'd been missing out on too much life, if one little hug and 2 minutes of hand holding felt like water to a person dying of thirst in a desert.

Before her stroke, Mom had tried to get her to date more, probably, so she wasn't always trying to handle life alone, but Diana had been very career-focused. Tears welled up in her eyes at the thought of her mom and the empty place losing her had left.

Sam did grab her hand, and his warm touch brought a watery smile to her face as they waited for Andrea to return with Linda.

"Miss Ramsey?" Andrea was back.

"Yes, I'm still here."

"I have Miss Linda on the phone. She'll be able to help you as much as anyone."

"I really appreciate it, Andrea. You're a gem."

"Hi Diana, Reagan talked so much about you. I feel like I already know you."

"Really?" Diana was surprised.

"Oh yes, she used to tell all kinds of wild stories about her aunt who liked to shoot guns and investigate insurance claims. The way she told it, you fought off three alligators and two looters to get to a house that had been damaged by a hurricane to expedite a claim for a lady who was 100 years old."

"I'm pretty sure it was three looters and two alligators, but yes."

She smiled at the astonished look on the guys' faces.

Linda was laughing.

"How can I help?"

"I remember Reagan talking about a friend from school who wasn't in the business. She loved to read, and they did several group projects together, but she said she was the biggest help with her grades and was the smartest kid in their class. A Hermione Granger type. Do you know who she was talking about?"

"Yes, actually. She got accepted to Harvard, so she's studying to be a lawyer. Her name is Tuyet Lopez."

"Great, if I give you my number, can you ask her to call me?"

"Sure, and I'm sure she would be happy to help. She was heartbroken when Reagan went missing and kept trying to say she wouldn't have run away. I know the school looked into it at the time. But they ended up coming to the same conclusion as everyone else did."

"How was Reagan as a student?" Diana asked. Desperate for more details about her life here.

"She was great, actually. Most kids who work in the entertainment business are very full of themselves. But Reagan would seek out the kids who were bullied by the others and befriend them."

"Really?"

"Yeah, she very easily could have been a popular, mean girl. But it was almost like she thought being in the entertainment business was silly rather than a social status accolade. I know she loved to read and worked very hard for her good grades."

Pride welled in Diana's heart at those words. It was something she knew was a big concern for her mom when Reagan would come to visit. That too much time in LA would turn her into a mean girl who would take for granted the people who struggled for a living.

"Thank you for sharing that. Just so you know, the team is here recording, and I wanted to ask if there is anything else you would want to share with the viewers about Reagan?" Diana asked.

"Yes, if anyone knows where this sweet girl is, tell her to come home. I know you miss her. But so do we, and Tuyet and I'm sure tons of other people who were lucky enough to know her. It's safe to come home now." She said,

Diana was surprised. Safe to come home was an interesting way to phrase that.

"Why did you say it's safe to come home now?" She asked bluntly.

"You must have met Layla at some point, right?" Her tone had shifted; it was harsher now.

"Sadly, yes. Sounds like you had a similar perception of her."

"Was there another perception to have? She tried to pull Reagan out of school to do content full-time. Reagan begged to stay. I had other students who would watch her content come to me with concerns over some of the grown men in her comment section who said the most vile things you can imagine."

"Yeah, I've seen some of those."

"It's disgusting."

"I agree. So you're thinking Layla was a problem?"

"A huge one to Reagan. Never enough for us to get CPS involved, but just a lot of very questionable choices and always a lack of concern."

"Can you give me anything specific?" Diana needed to know where this thread led. The fact that the teacher had mentioned it meant something. It was one of those random details people threw in, not thinking much of it, but it was their subconscious trying to alert them to something.

"I know it's gonna sound weird, but her prom dress."

"She was only 15. I thought Prom was for Juniors and Seniors?"

"Typically, but if a sophomore gets asked by a Junior or Senior, they can go, she was. Her prom dress looked like something an adult would wear to a club. Typically, I would have thought it was the kid pushing the boundaries, but I noticed as soon as she got inside after their pictures, she used her date's jacket to cover up and kept pulling the hem down."

"The guy she was with…"

"He was gay, so it wasn't like that, but it was clearly all done for the production of it all."

"Ok, thank you. But here's my number. Please have Tuyet call me as soon as possible."

"Were there any other friends who may know something?" Sam asked.

"I'm not sure. Tuyet may have a couple of suggestions. I didn't get the feeling she let many get that close to her."

"Yeah... I think you're right. Thank you." Diana whispered.

"I'll try to reach Tuyet as soon as I hang up. Good luck. I hope you find her and that she's safe."

"Me too."

Diana hung up the phone and noticed Sam was still holding her hand.

Brent made a throat-clearing noise and pointed at DeMarcus with the camera, and he almost reluctantly released it and sat back up to ask her.

"We got a name. That is a great step forward. How are you feeling?"

"A lot more hopeful than I was half an hour ago. But honestly, it was so nice getting to talk to other people who knew her. Her kindness, her empathy for others. That is how we knew her to be," Diana said, wiping a tear away before continuing.

"We'd always spend a day volunteering at the animal shelter when she would come to visit. Her mom was allergic, so she never got to have a pet. And she had helped me babysit Ray and Traci's kids before. She was always so kind to everyone."

Diana wiped another tear from her eye.

"How long do you think it'll be before you get the call from her friend?"

As soon as the words left his mouth, the phone rang.

"Hopefully, the 90 seconds since I hung up with Linda."

"Hello?"

"Hey, Diana. It's Pete."

"Hello Pete," There was no friendliness in her tone this time.

"I assume you've talked to the police up there by now..." He said hesitantly.

"Yes," she said, not giving him anything.

There was an awkward pause. She let it drag out on purpose.

"...Great, did y'all release something already?" He got straight to the point.

"Yes, the teaser for the first episode."

"Listen, Diana. I'm sorry it had to be this way. But I got worried about your safety after that biker was following you with stolen plates. I felt like I had to do something to get you out of dodge."

"Oh..." Diana didn't know what to say. She'd almost forgotten about the biker since nothing really had happened, but you know it was kind of weird how many things had happened to her while she was in L.A.. The robber, the biker, the other weird things. Maybe there was something going on.

"So listen, the reason I'm calling is the phone lines have been blowing up around here, and my captain spent all morning yelling at me, and I figured you may know why."

"Why are they calling you guys?" She asked. Hoping some of what was being said was useful. Knowing enough to know, most of it was likely bullshit.

"With tips, most of them seem fake as hell, but it's gonna take a hell of a lot of manpower to sort through it all, but I wanted to let you know we're doing it. We're putting resources into re-investigating the case."

Diana was still pissed at him, but this was good news; this was him saying they're not just paying her lip service. That they were doing everything they could.

So she decided to throw him a bone of a sort.

"Well, I have news to share, too. I just talked to her teacher, who knew of a friend from school who is hopefully gonna call me back with more leads to follow."

"That's something." He said, sounding hopeful.

"And this trip isn't a total loss. I wish you had told us what you knew so we could have made an informed choice. But I have to say, I'm disappointed in you, Pete."

"I can understand how you feel that way, but I'm sure your friend Ray and even Sam would have likely done the same thing if it meant keeping you safe."

"That's besides the point. I'm a big girl and I can handle it. Just no more wild goose chases. We're on the same side, and I'm not here to get in your way."

"Understood, so tell me what else you've found up there."

"Not much. Although I am wondering why they would pay for a cabin and then never show up."

"I'm not sure. Any number of things could have happened to them between here and there. Right now, we need to learn what the motive is. We no longer believe she ran away. So what other options does that leave us? An accident, or someone, took her against her will. Right?"

"Yeah, I guess if they had a car accident, it's possible for them to have drowned or something in a lake or a river. But if it was a kidnapping, she could be anywhere."

"Well, let's not get ahead of ourselves. We can identify bodies of water by I-5 and have dive teams go out if we run out of other leads to chase. But sadly, it looks like we're waiting on the phone to ring to know what's gonna be the best option."

"Yeah, I guess so."

"So are y'all coming back to L.A.?" Pete asked.

"I don't know yet. I felt like, since we know she was driving north on that last video, we're in the right neck of the woods. So we're gonna be here at the hotel in Ashland at least another day. Hopefully, Tuyet will call before too long."

"Hopefully. Keep me posted. And stay safe. Just remember, wherever you go, if someone did intentionally take her, you get too close to the truth. It can turn dangerous."

"Not to worry, we stocked up on some supplies before we left town, and you've seen my work. I'm no damsel in distress."

"I got that message loud and clear, but I mean for Sam and the others, you'll need to watch their backs, too."

They chuckled. Sam rolled his eyes.

"Don't worry, I will."

She hung up and looked at Sam. His face was unamused.

"We can cut that part," Diana teased.

"I personally thought it was great," Brent said.

"Well, it's about lunchtime. I know we got in late and got up early. I'm voting for food and a nap while we wait for the phone to ring," Diana said.

"Sounds good."

Chapter 15

DeMarcus ordered room service for everyone, while Brent and Sam went to Brent's room to do some work for the podcast. Media requests were coming in and although he didn't say it. Diana felt like they were going to work out how to respond to his ex's hit piece.

"Reagan sounds like she was pretty cool," DeMarcus said, handing her the food that had arrived.

"Yeah, she was. I'm sorry I kind of lost it at the police station."

"Don't apologize for that. It was real, and we all felt for you. I'm pretty sure Brent was crying."

Diana smiled at that thought. Knowing all of them were sharing this journey with her meant a lot.

"He is a big ole softy."

"Yeah, he is. And so is Sam when it comes to you. I've never seen him like this."

"Like what?" Diana tried to act innocent, but she could tell from DeMarcus's face that they weren't hiding anything about the way they were starting to feel about each other.

"... Affectionate, for one...I think he really likes you."

"What are we in middle school? Are you gonna ask me if I like him back? Where's the note you're supposed to pass that has the check, yes or no box on it?" Diana teased.

DeMarcus blushed.

"But seriously. I lost my brother a few years ago in a robbery gone wrong, and so I've been through this before. It really tore my whole family up."

"I'm so sorry for your loss."

"Thank you. That's actually how the family got to be so close with Sam. He helped keep pressure on the police with the articles he was writing until they arrested the killer."

"Are you trying to tell me that underneath his asshole layer, he's a good dude?"

"I'm sure you've already seen that his asshole layer is pretty much like camouflage. He is a good dude, through and through."

"You're a good friend, DeMarcus."

"I know." He said, turning to leave, but an idea struck.

"Hey, if you want to be a good friend to Sam. I wanna talk to your mom."

"Why?"

"To tell her how great you're doing. Moms love to hear people brag about their children."

"Sam is right. You're a terrible liar. This is about Beth." DeMarcus said with a grin.

"Dammit, were you watching the cameras from the car ride?"

"It is kind of my job," he gave with a knowing smirk.

This kid was a rascal.

"Listen, he made me promise not to mail her anything or spend money. All I want is her email, so I can use it to sign her up for every spam service I can find. She looks like she needs to be added to a few email lists so she can save money on her car's extended warranty!" He was laughing all the way out into the hallway, ignoring her request.

And now Diana was alone with her thoughts.

So many of them now were about Sam. The rising temptation to throw caution to the wind and dive into something with him both feet forward was hard to ignore.

But as she pulled out that last photo of Reagan, and remembered the little girl who needed her so badly. There was a looming feeling that she was becoming increasingly sure was true, she was already too late to save.

God, she missed her mom. Her dry humor and years of wisdom would have really been useful right about now. She was a hopeless romantic, so she knew which thoughts she would encourage. She could almost imagine how it would have gone if she'd brought Sam home to meet her one day.

Her inappropriate Southern Sass would have them all in stitches within minutes.

Diana finished her meal and was deciding on whether to take a nap, or watch more of Reagan's videos. Still wanting to do something that may be helpful. When her phone rang again.

"Hello?" she answered, putting the call on speaker and quickly walking across the hallway to Brent's room, where the guys were working. She noticed before he minimized the screen, she'd be right. It was an official response to Beth's article.

"Hello? Is this Diana Ramsey?"

"Yes, it is."

"Hi, this is Tuyet Lopez. I got a message you wanted me to call to talk about Reagan?"

"Yes, thank you for calling me back so quickly." She said as she waved at them to look at her phone. DeMarcus, with a half-eaten sandwich in his mouth, quickly pulled out his phone to record.

"Of course. I wish I had tracked you down sooner, but life..."

"It's ok. I know if we knew half of what we knew back then, a whole lot of things would have been different."

"What have you found out that we didn't know?" Tuyet asked.

"Well, for one, the so-called last video of her at the Santa Monica Pier was actually shot the week before, and her real last video showed her on a road trip to Oregon."

"Really? That's strange."

"Did she mention a trip to Oregon?"

"No, not Oregon. She knew for spring break they had booked a cabin in Northern California, but I don't remember her ever mentioning going as far as Oregon."

"Really...well that's... odd." Diana was dumbfounded.

"Yeah."

"Why would Layla's boyfriend book a cabin in Oregon but not plan to leave the state?"

"Was he laying a false trail?" Tuyet suggested.

Diana's eyes went wide... of course, the shady ass boyfriend! Then a thought occurred to her.

"Tuyet, you may have just cracked this case wide open! Thank you, thank you. I need to make a phone call."

"Please go, do what you need to do. Find her!" Tuyet said before hanging up.

Diana quickly dialed Sergeant Wickham.

He answered on the third ring.

"Pete. Pete.."

"What's wrong?" He asked. His concern was evident.

"They were never going to Oregon. It was a false trail."

"What?"

"Her friend called me back. Reagan had told her the cabin was in Northern California. It would explain why they were no shows. It was to plant a false trail."

"Is she sure she remembered correctly? It's been 5 years."

"This girl is at Harvard Law School. I would trust her memory," Diana assured him.

"So we need to find the real cabin they were going to. I can comb back through his financials and see if anything else pops up."

"No, look at Layla. I wasn't the only one who thought she was a piece of work. You had video of her being the one who actually took the money. What was the timestamp on that?"

"It was the 19th, at 8 am, when the bank opened. Why?" Wickham asked.

"Because I don't think Layla had time to get from where they took Reagan and make it back to the bank in time. Which means she planned this."

"Why would she plan to kidnap her own daughter?"

"I'm just spit-balling here, but it could be because she was trying to get Reagan to quit school and do content full time."

Sam interjected. "And her co-star Bailey mentioned only doing content to pay off the family farm and had quit shortly after Reagan went missing.

Maybe Reagan wanted to quit, too."

"And she was really focusing on her studies, according to her teacher," Diana added.

"All very plausible. It's a great working theory, but we need concrete evidence." Wickham said.

They all took a deep breath.

"I know. We just need to start over fresh. This time with a new perspective and with all the pieces of the puzzle on the table, so we can look again at how they fit together." Diana concluded.

"Very smart. Just please promise me you'll be careful." Wickham pleaded.

"We promise. And we'll keep you updated before we do anything. We will probably need your help again soon."

Diana hung up the phone and turned to Sam.

"Pull up that last video again. I want to have DeMarcus watch it."

"Really, why?" he asked.

"I noticed you're really sharp with cameras, and I'm guessing you haven't watched it closely."

"Sure, I'll take a look. I think I saw it once from across the room, but you're right, I haven't watched it closely." He said with a smile.

"I noticed you had moved the camera when you caught me crying one time during that interview with Bailey. You'd used the camera to track and followed a tear down my cheek in episode one. It was very cinematic. That's a crazy level of attention to detail."

"Ahh. Thank you." DeMarcus said bashfully.

They play the road trip clip again..

"That's Mt. Shasta." She pointed it out in the distance.

Right about the time it comes into view, the camera turns to face Reagan, who throws up a peace sign before ending the clip.

"There," DeMarcus says, pointing at the screen.

"There, what?" Diana asked him.

"The turn signal was on." He responded, pointing again.

"...It was?" Diana asks. The excitement was building inside of her.

"Yeah, you can catch a glimpse of it as she turns the camera around. I think they were getting off that exit."

"Quick, pull up Google Maps," Diana told Brent, who was sitting at the computer.

They line up the angles of the road to where they think that point of view would be possible, and then go to the street view to confirm. They find exit 729.

"That's just north of Dunsmuir," Brent said. His face was pale. The idea we drove right past there on the way to Ashland must make him feel like kicking himself, too. Diana thought.

"How far is that from here?" Sam asked.

"Hour and a half..." Brent replied, pulling up Google Maps.

"Let's go. Bring all the stuff, but we won't check out. Maybe we'll be back tonight, maybe not. But we're not waiting to find answers." Sam said.

"We should do another sit-down interview first," Brent suggested.

Everyone looked at him like he'd grown another head.

"I mean, this excitement you both have would be a golden opportunity to capture." He clarified.

"We'll do it in the car on the way," Sam said, taking Diana's hand and heading back to their rooms to pack.

Again, one of the tires was flat, and this time, it was the Tacoma. But they had insisted on getting a spare with this rental. The guys worked to change it. Diana took a moment to text Ray and Traci about the update. Diana was too excited to get to Dunsmuir to worry about yet another flat tire and what it might mean. If someone was trying to sabotage their investigation or throw her off wanting answers. She was happy to disappoint them. She was almost looking forward to them underestimating her. But looking over at Sam and how his eyes kept finding hers, she knew.

He would probably be upset if she told him she was feeling about as reckless as she had the night he found her in the bar. Pretending to be lured to the parking lot by some creep.

They finally got on the road. There wasn't a lot of chatting in the car. Every now and then, Sam would give her a look when she'd sigh as her thoughts started to drift. What if this was another wild goose chase? Eventually, he just asked.

"What's wrong?"

"I'm just worried it's another dead end." She said, voicing the fear she was feeling.

"Even if it is, we'll find another lead." He said, patting her on the hand. And then it lingered there, holding hers.

It's warmth giving her comfort.

"You know I kind of like this," Diana said, holding up his hand.

"Me too." He said with a small smile.

He took her hand to his mouth and kissed her knuckles gently where he had bandaged them, in a very sweet, tender gesture.

Diana's heart skipped a beat, but she reminded herself this was not the time.

To focus on something she could pursue, Diana decided to start filtering through more of the comments on the social media post.

"I just had a really random thought." She told Sam.

"What's that?"

"Other than checking in with the police, where are we going to look?"

"I just figured we'd talk to locals who were there back then to see if they happened to remember anything."

"Yeah, that was my first thought, too, but I was just thinking about that Mexico comment. I wonder if I can use a word search filter and see if someone had mentioned Dunsmuir that could give us clues."

"That's a fantastic idea." He said with a smile.

"Other than doing CTRL F on a website, I have no idea how to do a search for specific words on comments like that."

Sam shrugged at her.

"Copy and paste all the comments into a Word document. I'm not sure of an easier way." He said.

"That will work!" She responded excitedly.

"DeMarcus is our Gen Z tech wizard, but he's driving for Brent, so that's the best help I can give."

"I know, our old Millennial asses haven't kept up with all these newfangled gadgets as much as we thought we would growing up, did we?" she said with a smile.

"Not at all, actually. I long for the simple things now," He responded with a long look.

Yeah, simple things, like you and me and a bed with no responsibilities. Diana thought for a moment before returning to her task.

She pulled out her laptop. After a few minutes of finding the post with the most comments, she followed his suggestion of copying and pasting it into a Word document.

"Ok, moment of truth." She said as she pressed Enter.

The little box near the top of her screen came back with one result for Dunsmuir, and the screen flashed to the comment it highlighted.

Stacy Rae: They need to be looking in Dunsmuir.

"Oh my god! There's a comment about Dunsmuir." She could barely contain her squeal of excitement.

"Really? By whom?"

"Someone named Stacy Rae. I'm gonna check out her profile."

After a few moments, the profile loaded. Everything was pretty generic.

"She's a local. She's a bartender at a place called the Dining Car Restaurant."

"Ok, let's go there first and just see what she has to say," Sam said,

Diana nodded, not wanting to waste a moment.

"Sure. And I'll text Pete to let him know what we've found."

Sam had an almost involuntary eye roll at mentioning Sergeant Wickham's name, but Diana just smiled. Hope was a powerful thing.

As they kept driving, Sam kept looking over at her, and it was distracting.

"So, you mentioned something on the phone about alligators...I'm just very curious what happened there?" He eventually asked.

'Oh, it's really not that impressive. I may have told Reagan a slightly altered version of the truth."

"So what happened?" He asked again.

"Well, before I got the job I have now, I was an insurance producer. Which is basically customer service, with an insurance license. And I kept getting these calls after a hurricane from a lady who was 100 years old. So much of the forms and stuff are online now, and she never learned how to use computers. So when she needed to file a claim on her house, which she had lived in her whole life, mind you. The swamp around her house was still flooded, and no one would go out there to get the ball rolling for her until the water receded."

"But let me guess, you did," Sam said with a small grin.

"Of course I did. It really wasn't that big of a deal. She was just down in Georgetown, so not too far from me. I borrowed Ray's boat. Although he says I stole it." She said,

"I had my gun, so I made up the part about the looter...Well, I mean, I did see some guys out there who could have been looters. I didn't ask, they didn't tell. I had my open carry holster on. They left me alone."

Sam was shaking his head. But she continued.

"And there was a moment when I was wading into her house to get the best pictures possible. I did see some alligators. So thinking quickly climbed on the roof to wait for them to pass, but no one was hurt, no gators wrestled."

He didn't look happy. It was honestly a little nice to see someone a bit concerned about her welfare.

"The worst thing I did that day was forget the bug spray. I was eaten up with mosquito bites by the time I got home."

Sam looked like he wanted to disapprove. His eyes rolling, but a grin tugging at his mouth. However, he asked.

"But the lady was helped?"

"Of course she was. We got her claim processed and money paid out in like a week, and I got promoted."

He smiled and shook his head. She could hear him mutter "reckless" under his breath. But she decided to take it as a compliment.

Chapter 16

They arrived at the Dining Car Restaurant and walked inside. DeMarcus had suggested he and Brent stay back, so as not to spook her. Because she'd only left a comment. If she really wanted to be on the podcast, she would have called into their tip line. They didn't want to mess this up.

The lady from the profile had striking pink hair and was easy to spot behind the counter, and Diana felt like maybe their luck was finally changing for the better.

"Are you Stacy Rae?" she asked.

Shock washed over the bartender's face as she recognized Diana and Sam.

"Oh my god, y'all saw my comment?"

"Yes, we did," Diana told her with a smile.

"You remember seeing my niece all those years ago?"

"Yeah, she tried to pass me a fake ID, and I recognized her; my little sister was a fan. I saw you guys were looking into her case. I thought it may be helpful... Although I don't think I ever imagined you'd see it."

"Do you remember if she was with anyone like her mom?' Diana asked, getting her back on topic. There was not going to be any rapport building here. She could tell.

"No, I remember her being alone."

"Really?" Diana was starting to lose hope. Maybe this would not be the smoking gun clue they had hoped it would be.

"But you know I'm really glad you're here, because this has been weighing on me for years." The bartender looked mournful and couldn't look Diana in the eye anymore. Her hands were fidgeting.

"What?"

"Well, I just feel like it's a sign from God, you finding your way here. Just what, an hour after I made that post? I need to get it off my chest. To tell you what I know, even though I promised I would never tell anyone." She was almost in tears now.

Diana was torn between wanting to comfort her and shake her. For God's sakes, spit it out.

"I know what happened to her."

Diana's heart was pounding in her ears, and Sam grabbed her hand at the next words.

"After I refused her at the bar, back then I was barely old enough to drink myself, and never saw the harm in it. I mentioned where she could go to have a good time, and I'm afraid I sent that girl to her death."

"What do you mean?" Diana was about to lose control and attack this woman. Her voice was barely above a deadly whisper.

"It was spring break, and the guy I was dating had a group of friends in town. And he had texted me that they were looking for girls to party with that night. And if I saw anyone who looked fun, to send them their way."

"Can you give me names or an address?" Sam asked.

"Both. That fucker held a gun to my head and made me promise never to tell the cops what I knew. After it had been blasted all over the news, she was missing. But you know what? Fuck him, y'all ain't cops, and you have a right to know."

"All this time..." Diana started, but Sam cut her off and held onto her shoulders as she tried to take a step forward. The anger and rage she felt at how this bitch could know what she knew and keep her mouth shut for 5 goddamn years had her vision literally seeing red.

She had thought it was just an expression. It wasn't.

"Go wait outside. I'll get her to write down the name and address," Sam told her. Physically pushing her towards the door. Blocking her way to get to Stacy Rae.

She took a deep breath. Getting arrested for assault would delay finding the next clue. She turned on her heel and walked out.

She didn't know what had made Stacey keep her mouth shut all these years, and honestly, she didn't care. There was only finding the truth now to care about.

****

Sam quickly got the information he needed from Stacy and went back out to the Tahoe.

The sight that awaited him made Sam's heart stop beating.

DeMarcus lay crumpled on his side behind the truck, blood blooming beneath him like a spreading shadow. The knife, slick and glinting, had been discarded just out of reach.

"D!" Sam ran to him and dropped to his knees. He yanked off his button-down shirt and wadded it in his hands. He pressed it hard into the wound just below DeMarcus's ribs. The blood soaked into the material. Shit, Sam thought. He was losing a lot of blood.

"Who? Who did this?" His voice cracked. He wanted to scream, to tear the world in half, but his hands stayed steady.

DeMarcus coughed, blood bubbling at his lips.

"HELP!" Sam roared toward the diner. "SOMEONE HELP US!"

Sound warped, it felt like he was underwater. But then DeMarcus's lips moved.

One word. One name.

"Brent."

Sam's heart froze.

No. No, it couldn't be.

He looked up. No truck, no Diana, no Brent.

"Brent did this!" Sam shouted again, as if saying it out loud would undo it.

DeMarcus nodded weakly, and then his eyes rolled back.

"NO! Don't you do this!" Sam shook him gently, slapped his cheek. "Stay with me!"

The restaurant door slammed open behind him. Stacy bolted out, already screaming.

"He's been stabbed! Call 911!" Sam shouted.

"Oh my god, oh my god!"

"CALL. 911!" His voice cracked like thunder.

"Where's the nearest hospital?"

"North, Mt. Shasta. Off the I-5!"

"Help me get him in the car. Now!"

Adrenaline turned Sam into a machine. He lifted DeMarcus like he weighed nothing. He maneuvered him into the back of the Tahoe. The blood was everywhere.

"I'll hold pressure. You drive."

Stacy caught the keys, trembling. "Okay. Okay!"

Sam climbed in behind him, hands locked tight on the wound, his body shielding DeMarcus from every bump and turn.

"Don't you die on me. Don't you fucking die!" His voice cracked, low and desperate.

They hit the ER loading bay nine minutes later. Nurses and doctors swarmed like hornets. Hands grabbed DeMarcus. Voices barked questions. Sam's hands were still red when they pulled him away.

His blood type, who did this, and their relationship, but he needed to find Diana. The fact that she was in danger had him ready to rip his hair out. His panic had the words and thoughts coming out of him almost incoherently as he tried to answer their questions.

Luckily, there was a police officer stationed at the hospital who came over to question him.

Sam was pacing back and forth, not able to stand still.

"What happened to your friend?" He asked.

"He was stabbed. But he's here. We need to worry about my other friend, she's been kidnapped. The man who took her and did the stabbing. His name is Brent Humboldt. He was my employee."

"How do you know he did this?"

"DeMarcus told me his name before he lost consciousness. And Diana had just been with me inside the diner and stepped outside seconds before I did."

His heart was beating through his chest. He wanted to scream at the cop. To shake him. But he remembered something Diana had said once. You get more flies with honey than vinegar. She was rubbing off on him... God, he would not let her out of his sight again when he found her.

The cop seemed to be in zero hurry. Sam kept pacing back and forth. A million different thoughts running through his head. He started cycling between the facts. He would need to call DeMarcus's mom. Diana was in danger.

"What's their description?"

Diana is a beautiful redhead in her mid-thirties. She was wearing black pants, a white shirt, and a blue blazer. She is about five feet six inches tall and weighs 140 pounds.

"And he's your employee?" The cop said, writing down each detail in his little notebook.

"Yes, my producer. I run a true crime podcast. DeMarcus is also my employee. He does the camera. But Diana, we brought in for this case. She's the aunt of a missing girl we were trying to track down."

"Who's this missing girl?"

"Reagan Ramsey, she went missing 5 years ago.... Diana Ramsey is the missing woman."

"If you're running a true crime podcast, you think the niece went missing under suspicious circumstances?" He asked again. Not seeming to be in a hurry. Not even calling a BOLO over the radio so other cops could hear.

"Yes, you know what? This is taking too long. If you want the full back story, we've been working with LAPD Sergeant Wickham. He can help verify our story. Him and Detective Ashley Diaz. We need to find Diana."

"Do you know if they left in a vehicle or on foot?"

"Vehicle. It's a silver Toyota Tacoma. It's a Hertz rental from L.A.."

"Good, they'll have a record of the plate." Sam noticed his tone was calm... maybe it was a tactic to try to calm him down... it was having the opposite effect.

"Do you have any idea of where they would take her?" He asked, not even looking at him, just writing things down in his notebook. Sam wanted to throw the notebook across the room and shake the cop into doing something! Anything! He was over here acting like Barney fucking Fife, if Barney weighed close to 250lbs on a small 5'7 frame. He almost looked like a cartoon for donut-chasing cops.

"I have no clue. I don't even know … why he took her, or why he stabbed DeMarcus…unless?"

A vague thought entered his mind. It was something someone had said when he'd been doing research on serial killers for the Smiley Face case back in Chicago. They often try to insert themselves into the investigations. Maybe it was also true for cases like this.

"I need to see a picture of Keith Novack. I know he's been arrested before; you should have a mugshot in the system."

"Who's Keith Novack?" The officer asks.

"He was Reagan's mom's boyfriend and the guy we believe brought her up here."

"So he's a suspect?" It was almost comical how slow this guy was.

"Yes, and also in her mom's death as well. Layla Ramsey died two months ago from an overdose. A neighbor said they thought they saw Keith turn back up." Sam said, remembering some of the information they'd been told about him.

The officer went to his laptop and pulled up the mugshot. A picture he'd seen once before during research, but hadn't looked closely at before.

It's hard to tell if that was Brent. Brent was a lot heavier than this guy, who was muscular and 20 years younger in looks. The difference was shocking. Almost like Colin Farrell as he normally looked, and how he looked as the Penguin.

Then he noticed a scar on Brent's eyebrow that was pretty distinctive, and he knew. Brent Humboldt was Keith Novack. Shock made him stop breathing for a moment.

"He'd been recommended by one of my sponsors. He was their uncle, they said. He had a giant sob story about his wife cheating on him and leaving him… God damn it! I think he told me that on purpose for sympathy!" Because it was so similar to what had happened to him with Beth.

Brent had played him like a goddamned fiddle.

Sam wanted to drive his fist through the wall. He put Diana in danger by hiring the fucking kidnapper for his fucking podcast, and he never saw it coming.

A spider indeed, and now they've all been caught in his web.

He took a deep breath.

"Ok, I will deal with that later. Right now, we need to focus on finding Diana." He told the cop.

The cop still didn't call out her information over the radio. Sam didn't know why, but his brain was trying to warn him. Where was that feeling when all the times he had talked to Brent, and made up some excuse for him about being older or new, or just...grrrrrrrrr. He mentally groaned.

Pull yourself together, Samuel. He told himself.

Think, where would he have taken her...probably the same place they took Reagan.

"I have a clue. It may be a wild goose chase, but I think we should check it out."

"Ok, I'm listening?" The deputy said.

"We'd tracked Reagan's disappearance to here. And met someone who remembers seeing her in town before she went missing. They gave me a name and the address of the house she was last known to visit. Can we go check it out? Maybe if Brent is Keith, and he had something to do with Reagan's disappearance, that's where he took Diana."

"Sure, what's the name and the address?"

Sam looked at the little piece of napkin Stacy had written on.

"Harry Jepsen and 421 Patricia Lane in Dunsmuir."

That's when Sam noticed the name tag on the officer's uniform.

"H. Jepsen."

Shock dawned in Sam's mind...this cop was the guy!

Then the officer noticed he noticed his name, as they stared at the napkin, and Sam watched horrified. Almost in slow motion, as his pen clicked closed with deliberate calm. The friendly officer's smile drained away. In its place, something colder. It was clear he was done pretending.

"Whelp, sir, I'm gonna have to take you into custody now." He said, standing up. The glint in his eye was almost egging Sam to try to make a scene, so he could invent an officer-involved shooting, or something else that would justify tying up the loose end Sam had just unwittingly become.

Sam looked around for a way out. But the waiting room was empty, and most of the staff were in the back, trying to save DeMarcus. Resisting would be futile, and running as well. He'd then be a fugitive, likely blamed for the stabbing.

There was only one hope left. If this guy was involved. Either he'd be killed quickly. Or maybe, if there was a God, he would be taken to the same place they took Diana. He thought grimly as the cuffs clicked onto his wrists. But then, at least, he'd get to see her one last time.

Chapter 17

Diana woke up with a start.

Where was she? It was dark, damp, and musty-smelling. Cracks of light shone through small holes in the wall, helping her to identify that she was in some sort of shed.

The back of her head pounded. She'd been hit hard. But they didn't kill her, so although grateful, that was a huge cause for concern. Her hands were bound, and so were her ankles. She couldn't really tell with what exactly. Tape? There was a telltale pull at the hair around her wrist that told her it was a strong possibility.

As far as she could tell, it was a big shed. Possibly used for farming or working on cars. It was impossible to tell how much time had passed. She wasn't hungry and didn't have to pee, so she told herself it wasn't likely very long.

The memory of what had happened started coming back to her.

They'd been at the diner. She walked outside and saw Brent's eager face... and told him. "We think we know where they took her!" And she went to jump into the driver's seat so she could pull out in a hurry. Sam drove too safely for how she was feeling currently. That's when she saw DeMarcus on the far side of the Tahoe with a knife sticking out of his belly. And then...nothing.

Her brain wasn't registering what it was trying to tell her. But Brent's eager face kept floating behind her closed eyes as tears welled.

That poor kid. He was only like 21. About the same age as Reagan. His life had barely begun, and he may die because of her trying to find answers.

"Deal with that later." She told herself out loud.

Right now, she needed to get herself free of her bindings.

Her hands were luckily bound in front of her, and with her legs tied, she could scoot around a little. She found enough room to reach into her back pocket and see if anything she'd armed herself with had been left behind. Her hands brush across the flashlight.

"Thank god!" she whispered to herself.

She was able to get it out of her back pocket, but it fell behind her. More scooting around and fumbling in the darkness until she found it again and turned it on.

"Ok, just storage." She said, looking at the piles of stuff lying around.

Lumber buckets, old furniture. She put the flashlight in her mouth to get a better look at her bindings.

Duct Tape. Ok, I just need something sharp. She thought to herself.

She didn't want to try standing with her feet bound; hitting her head again would be a disaster. She spotted a saw blade in the distance in a stack of boxes high on top of a desk.

Diana scooted over to where the desk was.

She used the table to brace and pull herself up to a standing position. Carefully, without knocking everything over, got the saw out of the box and sat back down with it.

She carefully cut through the tape at her feet and then stood up. Now she placed the saw between her legs to hold it steady as she cut her hands free.

Great step one is complete. Now, step two: escape.

Should I escape, or should I wait for him to return, then attack? You're assuming he's gonna return and didn't just leave you here to rot? She argued with herself.

She went to brush herself off, and that's when she felt it.

He hadn't checked her thoroughly because he didn't catch the knife she had on a lanyard under her shirt. She pulled it out. Feeling better and more prepared, she went to the door, but it was locked.

OK, this is cheap metal. Maybe I can break the wall? She returned to the lumber, wondering if she could find a sturdy piece of wood.

That'll create noise. Maybe I need to be quiet? Or I'll alert them to my escape. The fear of making the wrong choice was almost paralyzing. Knowing it was all basically a 50/50 chance that she would make it out of this alive. But any choice was better than no choice, so she picked up a 4x4 piece of lumber.

The vantage point of where it was found showed her that the back wall behind the lumber pile had actually rusted away. She moved some more of the lumber to access the hole. It was small. Maybe half the size of a doggie door. Nothing bigger than a rabbit would fit through that. She thought. But pushing on it revealed the metal to be compromised, and it bent outward. Feeling excited, she kept applying steady pressure, and it kept moving. Enough for her to stick her head out and look around.

The sun was still out, but it was hanging lower than it was when they arrived in town around 3 pm. If she had to guess, it was maybe 4 or 5. But not 6 because it would be really setting by then and dark by 8.

"Think skinny thoughts, think skinny thoughts," she whispered to herself as she army crawled her way out of the tiny hole, the metal starting to groan at the pressure for her shoulders and then her hips. But she made it.

The back of the shed was at a tree line. She couldn't see any buildings around her, but could hear water.

She tried to make herself small and made for the tree line. Knees bent to keep herself low, in a fast duck walk.

The smell of the forest was sharp and earthy. She tried to make sure her feet didn't make sounds on the leaves beneath her boots.

Once she felt like she was a safe enough distance from the shed, she looked back. The shed was next to a house that looked like it was at the end of a dead-end street.

The urge to be violently sick was strong, but she shoved it down. Focus, survive first, then fall apart. She told herself. She was running on pure instinct, which was hopefully sharp enough to survive this.

The running water she could hear further into the woods must be a river. She figured it was likely the Sacramento River that ran along the I-5 near Dunsmuir. But which direction to head in was impossible to know.

However, she didn't have long to wait before a cop car pulled up next to the shed. She took a few steps forward to run towards safety. When she saw the cop pull Sam out of the back seat. His hands were handcuffed behind him. He looked heartbroken.

She hesitated at that body language. Why was he in cuffs? Was he in on it with Brent? Her mind immediately dismissed that. Brent obviously had something to do with Reagan's disappearance, and Sam wouldn't have investigated the case and brought so much attention to it if he'd been involved.

No... this was because he thought they were going to die.

The dress shirt he'd been wearing earlier was gone. Now it was just his tank top. Brent came out of the back porch of the house, and she could see him talking to the cop, but she couldn't make out what they were saying.

The cop gestured to the shed, and Brent fumbled some keys out of his pocket and then started walking to the locked door.

The cop then started marching Sam into the woods to her left at gunpoint.

Diana looked down. She was wearing a dark blue jacket, but her shirt and hair would give her away. She buttoned the jacket and knelt behind a tree to put her hair into a bun to minimize how much of it was visible.

The Cop and Sam were about 15 yards away from her in the woods when they heard Brent yell.

"She's gone!"

The cop stopped and looked back, dumbstruck. So did Sam, but he had a smile on his face. She even noticed some tears in his eyes when he thought she'd escaped.

"What do you mean, she's gone?" The cop yelled in a hushed tone. Clearly, there were neighbors about.

"I knocked her out, tied her up. Hands and feet both. Then locked the door. She must be a fucking Houdini."

"How far do you think she could have gone?"

Diana watched Sam. He wasn't fighting or resisting them. He needed her help. Sam was a big, strong guy. He probably didn't know the statistics of why you never let them take you to a secondary location.

"Who knows? It's been maybe an hour since I took her. But you haven't heard any traffic on your radio, right?"

"Yeah, not a peep. That bitch Stacy must have told them, but I bet she saw me at the hospital and ran. I saw her driving the vehicle they arrived in."

"So what do we do?" Brent asked him.

"We take care of him first, then you stay here and hide, and I go find her."
The cop sounded frustrated, and then he asked, "I still don't understand why
you didn't just kill her too?" Diana couldn't help but be curious about Brent's
answer.

"I'd been waiting this whole time to get her separated from Sam. The two
of them together would've overpowered me. I told you what happened with
that mugger you bribed," Brent said to Harry.

Diana's breath caught. She saw the shock she felt mirrored on Sam's face.
Brent had arranged that?

"It's just as well," the cop went on. "We cleaned up the operation just in
time. They were getting too close, too fast. But all's not lost. We can send her
with the others. When we grab her."

Others? What did that mean? What the hell was going on here? Diana
thought... worry about that later... step three...or was it four...whatever step
we're on now... rescue Sam.

"Move!" the cop yelled at Sam, forcing him to keep walking further into
the woods. They never looked at where she was hiding.

Diana followed as quietly as she could as they kept walking. Her heart was
beating through her chest. But her goal was to save Sam, and it was helping
to keep her focused.

She could hear them talking in more normal tones the further from the
house they got. It told her they were heading deeper into the forest.

"You know what's funny?" The cop asked Sam just before they got to the
river.

"You started this whole thing by looking into a missing girl's case. And now
you're about to die the same way she did."

The world seemed to stop around Diana.

"What do you mean?" She could hear Sam ask.

"That bitch put up so much of a fight at the little party we were having. Keith
here got over-stimulated and strangled her. We took her to this same spot,
hoping it would look like a waterfall accident. But it was her mom actually

161

who suggested listing her as a runaway."

"Her mom knew where she was?" Sam asked. Ever the investigator. God love him.

"Yeah, she was the one who had her brought to the party."

"You keep saying party, why do I get the feeling it means something different to you than it does to me?" Sam was again pushing for answers.

"Do you know how much money guys pay to fuck pretty young things like Reagan Ramsey?"

Sam shook his head.

"Take that number and 10x it, because it was fucking the famous Reagan Ramsey."

Diana's blood started to boil. She was going to murder every last one of them.

However, Sam didn't deserve to die. He was trying to get her answers. She didn't know if he'd seen her or knew that she was close. Or if he just really didn't know when to quit, but she was going to try to save him. She refused to lose him, too. Not today. She told herself with quiet determination.

"Yeah, that was all Layla," Brent said.

'What was all Layla?" Sam asked.

"She got Reagan into content creation to increase her value."

Sam turned back in disgust to look at Brent.. Keith, whatever his name was. Diana dipped behind a tree and started praying. Lord Jesus. Whatever level of hell you sent that woman to when she died, you need to 10x it.

"Yep. Genius of a woman, but she had to go when I heard you were looking into this case."

"You killed Layla?" Sam asked.

"Yep. Easier than you'd imagine. She never saw it coming."

She was running out of time to act. Think, what gives me the biggest advantage? she thought to herself.

Sam was being marched in front of the two of them. The cop had his gun out. It was a Glock 22, same as Ray's gun back home. A full-sized .40 typically holds 16+1 rounds.

She had a knife and a flashlight. But Brent wasn't unarmed either, thanks to her. And their little shopping trip to the gun store.

The cop seemed to be more in charge of the situation than Brent, even though he was the one who had done the two, maybe 3 murders if DeMarcus didn't make it. But Diana chose to hope that Sam was able to save him after the cop mentioned the hospital.

Could she get close enough behind him, without being seen, to slice his throat? The thought made her shudder. She looked at her flashlight.

Well, I'm only gonna get one chance at this. She thought. She threw the flashlight into the woods, away from her location and as intended. They stopped and looked off to the far right.

She walked as quietly as she could over the leaves and twigs. She held the knife in her left hand so she could use her right to go for the gun at the same time.

Just as they thought it was a bird or something and started moving again, she made her move.

Her arm snaked around his neck, finding the exposed skin while her right hand grabbed over the top of the slide of the Glock, forcing it down.

Warm blood started spilling across her left hand, and a round fired into the dirt behind Sam.

The sound echoed through the woods, but she barely noticed it as the adrenaline dumped into her system.

"RUN!" she yelled at Sam.

Sam rammed his shoulder into Brent, who stared at her dumbfounded. Brent landed on the ground.

She dropped the knife to focus on gaining control of the gun.

The cop's left hand came up to where her right hand was over the top of the slide around her wrist and used a judo move to flip her off his back.

She looked up to the barrel of his gun pointed at her head and saw, almost in slow motion, as he pulled the trigger at the same moment Sam's body crashed into hers to protect her.

Click.

Her hand had blocked the shell casing from ejecting on that first round. The gun had jammed.

The cop's training kicked in. She saw him move into a tap-rack-roll malfunction-clearing maneuver, and her vision began to tunnel, everything narrowing to the gun in his hand.

She rolled out from under Sam's weight and scrambled to her feet.

Sam rolled and lashed out with a kick to the cop's knee, throwing off his stance. Just enough. The shot went wide, inches from her shoulder.

She went for the gun in front of her with both hands. Forcing it up while bringing her knee to the cop's crotch.

Her breath came in gasps as she forced all her strength into fighting for control of the weapon.

He grunted but still maintained control.

Her hands were twisting the barrel, trying to remove it from his grasp. But he was stronger and had better training as a law enforcement officer.

Brent was slower, but was trying to get to his feet. Sam, now back on his feet, kicked him in the head with such force that he was out cold.

She kept fighting. Not letting go of the gun. Knowing from her friend Ray. Training to protect your gun was an area of police training they spent the most time on, so she tried to think what else could she do.

The wound on his neck was superficial at best, she could see now. If only she hadn't dropped her knife.

She leaned down and bit him on the nose.

"AHHHHHHHH" He was yelling.

His eyes were watering, his instinct to protect his face, battling with his training to protect his gun.

She kept driving her feet into the ground, pushing him back as he tried to keep her off his gun. A tree root ended up being what saved them. He fell backwards, his wrist connecting with a tree, helping her get enough torque to get the gun.

Now he was on his back, and she held the gun pointed at his head. She really wanted to pull the trigger, but she hesitated. Breathing hard. He had said Reagan was gone, but he knew the people they had tried to sell her to. She wanted to see all of them brought to justice.

"It's OVER!" she yelled.

He held his hands up to protect his face, clearly thinking she was about to end him.

"I am making a citizen's arrest."

Sam walked up next to her.

"Put your hands up." She told him he was on the ground on his back, so it did her no good. But she kept issuing clear commands, making sure he didn't go for his taser or pepper spray, and keep the fight going.

"Roll onto your stomach, keep your hands up. "

As soon as he was not looking at her, she took a step to the right.

She noticed a spare set of cuffs on his duty belt.

"Place your right hand on the back of your head. Use your left hand to remove those cuffs from your back."

He complied.

"Now put your left hand up at the back of your head."

He did, still holding the cuffs.

"Now cross your legs and lift them up."

This basically put him in a hogtie position, which is what she wanted.

Now he wouldn't be able to move without making major noticeable movements.

Cuffing him wouldn't be easy, but she got it done, and once that was done, she used the key to secure his cuffs and uncuff Sam.

He brought her into a crushing embrace. His hands framing her face.

"You saved me," he said, his voice raw, like he didn't fully believe it had happened.

Diana took a deep breath, fighting to keep control. She was trembling with adrenaline..

"Someone had to," she whispered.

Sam dipped his head and kissed her.

It wasn't soft. It was desperate.

A collision of fear, fury, and pent-up feeling that finally cracked the wall between them. His mouth was warm, the pressure firm, his hands ghosting over her cheeks like he needed to make sure she was real.

She kissed him back without thinking, letting it anchor her for just one heartbeat in the middle of chaos.

But the moment was fractured as Brent groaned behind them. Sam pulled away, breathless, his forehead resting against hers for a split second before reality snapped back into place.

"Cuff him," Diana said

Sam used the cuffs that had been on him to handcuff Brent.

"What now?" He asked.

"Well, we clearly can't call the local cops. So let's sit them down next to each other and think this through."

"Where's my phone?" Diana asked Brent.

"Mine's in the cop car," Sam said.

"Was there anyone else in that house?" Diana asked. They shook their heads, but Diana didn't know if she should believe them.

"I'm sure there was a rope in that shed they had me in. How about I hold them here at gunpoint and you go back, make sure they're telling the truth, get your phone and the rope and come back." She told Sam.

"Why do we need the rope?"

"Because I don't want them getting any bright ideas," Her tone, a warning.

"I don't know if I like leaving you alone out here." He said, looking around at the forest.

"It's maybe 100 yards. I'll be fine." She said, press checking to make sure there was a round in the chamber.

He kissed her again. Then again. As if once wasn't enough to convince himself she was still alive.

When he finally pulled back, his breath was ragged, his forehead pressing gently to hers like he couldn't quite let go.

"Don't ever do that again," he whispered, voice hoarse with something dangerously close to fear.

"What?" she asked, confused and breathless.

"Don't risk yourself like that. Not for me."

"Too late," she said, brushing the blood from his cheek with shaking fingers. "I'd do it again tomorrow."

His eyes shut for a beat too long, jaw clenched.

"That's what I'm afraid of," he said, his voice cracking as he stepped back, like it physically hurt to do so.

Then he turned, walking back toward the trail they'd come from, his shoulders tight.

She swallowed hard, forcing her focus to shift. The threat wasn't over. Not yet. Until those bastards were zip-tied to a tree or in the back of a patrol car, she couldn't afford to let her guard down.

He was back within minutes.

He wrapped the rope around their legs, making sure they weren't able to go anywhere. Then tied it off to a tree.

"Ok hold this, I'm gonna call Pete." She said, handing the gun to Sam. Her arms had been getting tired.

Diana couldn't help but ask Brent...Keith whoever he was. "Why did Layla do this to her own daughter?"

Brent looked at her, his face emotionless. He let out a sigh and then almost resignedly said.

"She always hated the kid. Your brother had convinced her to keep the pregnancy until it was too late to get an abortion. But she always blamed her for ruining her body and was, in my opinion, jealous of her."

"I just can't wrap my head around it."

"Few can," was all that he said.

Chapter 18

The immediate aftermath went by in a blur. Pete was able to send in the CHP to take control of the scene. Sam wasn't sure what he said to whom, but the cavalry showed up. By the time they arrived. Brent and the cop were ready to turn on each other to get the best deal.

He ended up having to talk to multiple cops, from multiple agencies, repeating the same story, and details over and over. Sam found it hard to keep his eyes from constantly returning to Diana as she was questioned closer to the shed. She showed the cops how she escaped. They found the saw and cut tape binding, and it corroborated their story.

Once released, a kind officer was willing to give them a ride to the hospital so they could get an update on DeMarcus.

Not knowing what they would find when they got there filled Sam with dread.

He walked inside, holding Diana's hand, and told the lady behind the counter they were there for DeMarcus.

"We'll have someone come get you." She said,

Sam brought Diana's hand up to his lips and kissed her knuckles. Still bruised from punching the tree. He needed that physical reminder that she was there and she was safe. The overwhelming fear he'd felt when she'd been taken still had not fully subsided.

Getting her to see things the same way he did regarding their future may be difficult. Maybe she would surprise him. Because he wouldn't blame her one bit if she didn't run straight back to South Carolina and never want to see him again. He'd nearly gotten her killed. And instead of reuniting her with

Reagan, all he'd done was help uncover a devastating truth. Reagan was gone. Diana hadn't even had time to grieve yet.

He worried she'd retreat into that hard shell of independence she wore like armor, trying to survive the loss alone. But he wasn't going to let her. Not this time. He was staying, however close she'd let him stand.

They were ushered into a smaller waiting room down the hall of the emergency department. He used this time to call DeMarcus's mom.

"Hi Doris, it's Sam."

"Hi Sam, how's it going out there?"

"Not good. DeMarcus has been ... injured."

"What do you mean DeMarcus has been injured?"

"He's been stabbed. We're at the hospital waiting for an update. I'm flying you out. I need you to head to the airport."

There was a scream on the other end of the phone, and Sam looked down in shame. After DeMarcus' brother Jayden had died, the thought of possibly being the reason she might be losing her other son was too much. Tears started rolling down Sam's face, and he took a shuddering breath as the weight of everything crashed around him.

Diana stopped pacing the waiting room and walked up to wrap her arms around him. His chin fitting just over her head.

Again, he was struck by how magnificent she was. To offer him comfort in a hug. After everything they'd been through today. All the danger he'd personally brought to her doorstep by not recognizing Brent for what he was.

"Tell me, is my boy alive?" Doris asked.

"I don't know. We're waiting for an update at the hospital now."

"Who did this?" She sobbed.

"Brent, the producer," Sam said coldly.

"Brent? DeMarcus said he was cool! What the hell happened?" She sounded like a wounded animal. Mirroring how he had felt when he'd learned the truth.

"Turns out Brent had been lying to us all. He was the criminal we'd been chasing. But we got him. He's in custody, and he will be going to jail for the rest of his life."

"I'm heading to the airport now. Book a flight for me and his sister Tasha

169

...where the hell are we going? DeMarcus said y'all were on the road a lot for this case."

"Mt. Shasta, CA. It's up north near the OR border, so bring a jacket."

The door opened, and the doctor came inside.

"Hang on, Doris, the doctor just arrived." He put the phone on speaker.

"This is his mother. How is he?" Diana said, pointing at the phone.

"He's doing better. You guys got him here pretty quickly, so we were able to get him into surgery. The knife wound perforated his small intestines and nicked the gallbladder. So, although there was a lot of blood and, as always, the risk of infection. The surgery went routinely, and we removed the gallbladder and repaired the intestines. He should make a full recovery. We'll want to keep him here for about a week, but he should be able to go home after that."

"Thank you, Doctor," Sam said. Relief washed over him. DeMarcus was like a little brother to him. Knowing he was ok made his knees weak.

Doris was crying on the phone.

"Doris, did you hear? He's ok." Sam croaked into the phone.

"Thank you, Jesus." She cried.

Diana hugged him tighter. He wrapped both his arms around her for a moment. Before bringing the phone back up to his ear.

"I'll email you your flight information. We'll pick you up from the airport. You'll be flying into Redding, CA."

"Thank you, Sam," she said, disconnecting.

"Can we see him?" Diana asked the doctor.

The doctor nodded and led them to the recovery room.

He was breathing on his own, but had tons of IVs and an oxygen cannula, and a drainage tube from his surgery.

"He'll be in the ICU to monitor him for the first 48 hrs, and then we should be able to move him to a regular room. Let me know if you guys have any questions. They'll be coming to move him to the ICU in about 30 minutes."

"Ok, thank you," Sam said.

"Oh my god, look at him!" Diana said tearfully. Walking up to DeMarcus in the hospital bed, running her hands through his hair.

"I know." Sam remained by the door.

"We all could have died today!" Diana choked out. Her body was visibly trembling.

Sam took it all in. It was over. The case was solved. The bad guys were on their way to jail. His tribe, wounded but alive.

This would take a lot of processing for them both. But the urge to be there for her. To make sure she was ok, moved him across the room, pulling her into his arms.

"I know." He kissed her forehead.

Sam spied a chair in the corner and made the quick decision to pick her up. One hand under her knees and the other supporting her back, and took the few steps to the chair to sit and settled her on his lap so he could cuddle her close. And relish in the fact that they were both alive.

"What are you doing?" Diana asked.

"You've had yourself a day. One day very soon, I plan to spoil the hell out of you to make up for everything my coming into your life has caused you."

Diana looked at him. He could feel her heart beating fast.

"Why?" she whispered.

Staring into her beautiful green eyes, he knew it was time to put words to the feelings that had been growing since the first time he met her.

"Because I'm not going to be able to just walk away from you." He took a deep breath and continued. "I can't just go back to my life the way it was before you. Like you had never set fire to my soul and woke me out of a mind-numbing petrification I'd been in for years. Existing but never really living."

Her eyes went round at his declarations.

"I know you probably want to run away and never see me again after everything, but I can't let you go. Not without telling you everything you have come to mean to me."

Her face was unreadable. He had no way of knowing how she was taking what he was saying, but he had to say it.

"I have cherished every moment I have spent with you, except about half of today when we were scared out of our minds that we were going to die. That I wouldn't like to do again. But it is my biggest hope that you let me spend the future cherishing you with all of the love in my heart."

Diana didn't move but continued to look at him, and panic started to set in. Had he scared her away? Had he lost her before he ever really had her?

It didn't matter; he would continue to love her regardless of how she felt about him. Like she called him once. He was a truth hunter, and the truth in his heart knew he would always love her.

"If you don't kiss him. I will," came a soft raspy voice from the bed.

DeMarcus was awake.

They both looked up at him to see him smiling at them.

Diana turned back to Sam, and she kissed him with heat and passion matching his own. Her lips were soft under his. Her hands framing his face.

Desire and hope crashed into him in equal parts. Desire at the fact that their spark was now a whole-ass flame. And hope that maybe, just maybe. She felt the same way he did.

Then she pulled back and looked at him.

"I want to make you a promise."

Sam could not expect the next words that came out of her mouth.

"I can't promise it will always be easy, or that I will never throw things at you again, but I do promise I will make it worth it. I'm all in. I love you."

A smile of joy and relief spread over his face.

"Jesus, get a room, you two," DeMarcus said.

A nurse came in and said in the most deadpan tone ever.

"They can have this one. Your room upstairs is ready."

Chapter 19

They look at each other and Diana can feel her heart thumping like it's about to beat out of her chest. The way Sam is looking at her. She knows he's considering the nurse's offer to use this room.

Hell, after what he said, he's lucky she hasn't ripped his clothes off of him. Yet, here and now isn't what either of them wants. She snuggled closer into his embrace, her head cradled in the curve of his neck as he just continued to hold her.

She couldn't help but notice he smelled like cotton and cedarwood.

"I'm so glad DeMarcus is ok," she said after a few minutes.

"I am too. But I am so sad about Reagan, baby. I know we've been avoiding talking about that since everything else happened. But I just wanted to be clear, whatever this podcast episode will be, will entirely be up to you. I'm gonna tear up that contract when we get back to the hotel."

Diana sat up and looked at him.

She had known in her heart. Ever since he showed her that picture at her house in Pawleys Island, she'd known. Because if it had been anything else that had happened, Reagan was strong and fierce and would have escaped and come and found her if she'd been alive.

"Her story deserves closure. But we can talk about that tomorrow. We should get going, though. They'll need this room, eventually."

"Yeah, we need to head back to the hotel."

"God, I hate being a responsible adult," Diana said as she carefully got off of Sam's lap.

He flashed a grin at her. It seemed to surprise him that, of all the things she could have said, he didn't expect that. Good. Need to keep him on his toes. God forbid he ever gets bored with her.

Her mom had told her since she was young that when you meet a good man, you don't let him go. And looking back at the time, she'd know Sam. Good barely scratched the surface. Principled, honest, tough, present. And the best bonus...affectionate.

"I know what you mean," He said, standing as well. He pulled her close to whisper in her ear.

"If I wasn't a responsible adult," he murmured, "I'd tell you exactly what I want to do to you right now. First, we would close the curtains around where DeMarcus's bed was, and then..." His lips started kissing a line from her cheek down her neck as she tried to string coherent words together.

"Well, there's nothing all that horizontal in here anymore, and neither that chair nor that wall will do. Guess you need to find me somewhere else where we can finish that thought."

She could feel him smile against her neck.

"As you wish."

The drive back to the hotel was quiet. Diana tried to stay awake. But the events of the day were catching up with her.

She woke up with a start when he parked the Tahoe back in Ashland.

"We're here." He said.

Diana yawned. "I must have dozed off."

He got out and went around to open her door. But instead of just opening her door, he swept her off her feet and carried her inside. Never setting her down once in the lobby, the hallway, or even the elevator.

Luckily, it was late, so other than the night clerk, no one else saw. Eventually, they reached the door, and because he refused to put her down even to open it, she had to awkwardly unlock it so he could carry her in and lay her on the king-sized bed.

"I'll be right back," Sam said, pressing a kiss to her forehead before slipping into the bathroom.

Diana lay back, the room dim and quiet, and not for the first time that day, the thoughts came. But this time, she was unable to suppress them.

Reagan.

The girl who used to burst into summer like she owned it, bare feet, wild laugh, eyes full of fire. She'd never be that girl again. And worse, she'd never become the woman she was meant to be.

Diana had avoided all of this by being practical. There were police to answer. Sam to worry about. DeMarcus's mother to call. Everything to do, everyone to protect. But that nap in the car had reset her body just enough to let the grief catch up.

Her heart felt like it had been ripped out and was only still beating because of Sam's confession of loving her. And finally, being able to admit the truth, she had fallen, too.

He'd slipped past her defenses. She hadn't meant to let him, but somewhere between guilt and determination, he'd gotten in.

And now that the case was over, now that the ending had come in the worst way possible, she was grateful he had. Because without him beside her, she might have shattered.

And as eager as she was to let him put her back together piece by piece. Not yet.

For one more night, she'd pretend to sleep.

Later, when Sam drifted off, she'd slip out of bed, pull out her phone, and scroll through every photo she had of Reagan. To say goodbye in her own way. Alone.

****

Nature's call sure had some shitty timing, Sam thought to himself as he returned to the bed to see that Diana had fallen back asleep.

Probably for the best. It had been a hell of a day. Plus, this would give him the chance to prove to her that he was serious. This wasn't casual for him.

So he climbed in beside her and held her close until he fell asleep as well.

At first, he thought he must be dreaming. But this wasn't a dream.

A sharp, involuntary intake of breath hitched in his throat as he opened his eyes to find Diana beneath the sheets, her warm breath brushing over him with intent.

Her eyes met his, wide and mischievous, and fully awake now.

"Morning," she whispered, her voice low and hoarse from sleep, but the look she gave him was anything but innocent. Sam's heart kicked into a full gallop. "Well, good morning to you too..."

"I got curious about all those promises you had been whispering about lately, and I was impatient. I hope you don't mind."

"Mind?" he groaned. "Sweetheart, I'm yours to do with as you please."

"What if what I want is to make you happy?" "She tugged his waistband down, freeing him with deliberate care."

"You really want to make me happy?" he asked, voice low.

She nodded without hesitation.

In one swift motion, he hooked a leg behind hers and rolled, flipping her onto her back and pinning her gently beneath him.

"Where the hell did that come from?" she laughed, breathless.

"I've got a few tricks up my sleeve," he said with a grin

"See, as a man in love, nothing will ever make me happier than seeing you be happy. So let me make you happy, baby."

His mouth kissed a trail of fire up her thigh until he was able to lay her bare beneath him.

He settled into position between her legs. And looked into her mossy green eyes, ready to plunge in, when she asked.

"Do you have a condom?"

"FUCK!"

He rolled off the bed and moved to the far side of the room from her.

"You're not on birth control?" He was astonished.

"No. It hasn't been a priority in a while since casual hookups aren't my thing. I always assumed that when I met a nice guy, I would have time to figure things out before we reached this stage. Never realized that almost dying made you rethink all of your life choices this much."

He snickered.

"Life choices...huh..." He was thinking about a few life choices and reckless actions he might be willing to risk with her in this moment.

He stared back at her, breathtakingly beautiful from across the room. Her milky white skin was dotted with freckles, and her red hair was tousled. She was almost irresistible.

But he knew he was playing the long game. And he needed her to know it, too. Which meant doing things the right way.

He changed up his game plan. He may not be able to get to home base this morning, but he could at least steal a few bases.

Epilogue

Diana couldn't believe how much her life had changed in 6 months. The horrors found in California now brought to light for the world to see.

Sergeant Wickham was now Lieutenant Wickham, having gotten a promotion for his work on their case. He and Detective Diaz were now testifying before a Grand Jury to get the formal indictments to bring Brently Keith Novack and Harry Jepsen to trial. The trial would take years. Their investigation so far had taken months to really get a full scope of how big this was.

Layla had orchestrated much of the abuse Reagan had suffered. Paper trails and evidence from the sponsor parties, and the guy who had been featured in the photo that had started this whole thing, had been discovered.

Text messages going back years had documented a lot of the abuse, and threats of stopping her annual trips to South Carolina if she ever acted out of line.

Her motive was apparently a mix of jealousy and greed. The more beautiful and popular Reagan got, the more vicious Layla got.

This is why with Reagan almost reaching the age of 16 where she could legally file for emancipation, and being encouraged by Bailey to get out of the business and put an end to Layla's money making operation had been the final straw.

Brent. Seemed to enjoy playing the mastermind. The challenge of keeping ahead of any investigation thrilled him more than the greed of how much money they were making on selling Reagan. Who had not been alone, as they found evidence that this also happened to several other up-and-coming influencers.

He really felt like an evil genius the more they uncovered about him. He had plotted the false trail to Oregon, and arranged her kidnapping with Harry Jepsen to look more like she had snuck off and got into trouble just in case Layla's runaway story didn't work out.

He'd then fled the area to the East Coast, where he eventually met Sam.

He'd seen an interview Sam did about how he found the cases he covers on the local news.

Sam had said. "There are millions of cases all over the country that never got the attention they needed in that first critical 48 hrs. Just yesterday my 16-year-old neighbor's kid was telling me about a YouTube child star that went missing 5 years ago, that everyone thought she ran away, but there was a thread on Reddit speculating that she never did. The information is out there if you know where to look."

"Is that the next case you're looking into?" The interviewer had asked.

"I'm not sure. I've got a lot of potential cases to work on next, but you never know. Reagan Ramsey, if you're watching this and want to not be considered missing anymore. Now would be a good time to say something before I do a bunch of work and find out you're flipping burgers in Iowa or something." He had said cheekily.

If only that had been her fate. But no. They found out a body had been recovered from the river 5 years ago and Officer Jepsen, motivated by greed, had swapped the DNA swabs, so the results never matched. This was the nail in his coffin as he'd been the officer on the chain of custody in that case. So the body was exhumed and retested.

It had confirmed Diana's worst fears. Reagan was gone, and she was truly alone in this world.

Well, not completely alone. She still had Ray and Traci. But now she also had Sam.

Today was not to focus on that, but to focus on remembering Reagan.

The turnout was massive for the funeral. They could finally have one now that the body had been released to them and transported cross-country. She walked to the front of the tiny beachfront church in Pawleys Island, her heels echoing against the worn wood floor.

Next to the podium stood a framed photo of Reagan. Grinning at the camera. Pink roses spilled around the base of the easel, soft and vibrant against the quiet. They'd been her favorite. As Reagan's last living relative, it was her job to deliver the eulogy.

"Reagan Amelia Ramsey was a vibrant, shining star in a world of darkness."

A tear ran down her cheek. This was going to be harder than she ever imagined.

"For years, she hid that darkness behind the light of her shining smile and good deeds. Yet darkness may have taken her from us. All of us gathered here today know, darkness will never stop the good she did, or the lives she touched, or the brightness she brought those who loved her."

She could see Sam in the crowd smiling, encouraging her to go on.

"I could not stop the darkness I had no idea existed for her. Yet I am happy to announce, and this time is as good as any, that justice I can bring. We just received word from Detective Diaz that the Grand Jury has returned a true bill and the people responsible for taking this sweet girl from us are going to trial."

There was a cheer in the crowd.

"So I want to encourage everyone to remember the lesson Reagan so valiantly taught us. No matter the darkness. Bring light to others, and know there is help out there. Reagan, my sweet girl. We love you and hope you are finally at rest. And you will live forever in my heart."

And with that, she stepped down while people stood and cheered and clapped, and she returned to Sam's side.

The funeral eventually ended, and as Sam drove her home, he leaned over and grabbed her hand to pull it over and kiss the back of it.

"You did great today."

"Thank you. It's been a long day."

"Well, there's something I've been wanting to talk to you about, and I wasn't sure how to bring it up."

"What's that?" Diana was surprised.

"Well, although it pains me a lot to say this. I don't think we ever would have solved this case without you."

"Well, in the spirit of being honest. I'm not sure how you solved any cases before you met me."

Sam gave her a look at this quip.

"Well, if you're up for it and would be willing to do it. I want to offer you a job."

"A job?"

"Yes. I want to travel the world and solve missing persons and murder cases with you."

Diana's heart squeezed. Her job had let her take an extended absence due to the circumstances of what had happened in California, but she had bills to pay and had started working again after a few weeks off. Her time apart from Sam had been hard. But being able to pay her bills and return to a sense of normalcy had been important. However, she had gotten used to having him around. When he could be there. He was front row in L.A. for as much as he could be, making sure the police checked every box, crossed every T, and dotted every I so there was no chance at all Brent or Jepsen would ever see the light of day.

"Really, and what kind of benefits would this job come with?"

"Well, you get to make your own schedule. You get to pick 50% of the cases we cover, and me. You get all of me."

"That does sound nice."

"No, I mean it. You get all of me. Diana. I love you. Will you marry me?" He said, holding up a ring for her. Right here in the middle of traffic, this man couldn't even wait till they got home to ask this. This was so like him. This was his truth, and he had to say it.

A slow smile spread over her face.

"Of course I will. I love you too, and I accept your job offers. For co-host and wife."

She leaned over the console of the car and kissed him until someone behind them honked.

And she thought to herself as he pulled into her driveway and insisted on carrying her in from the car and over the threshold.

She may have buried the last of her family today. But she was going to start a new branch on the family tree with him, and looking back at how it all really happened. It was the most beautiful gift Reagan could have given her from beyond the grave. Diana was sure it was Reagan who really and truly brought her Sam.

Bonus Chapter: The Podcast

"Thank you for joining us on Second Look Cases. I am your host, Sam Benson, and this is my new Co-Host, Diana Ramsey." He said into the microphone at the round table they had set up to do the final episode for Reagan's case.

"Happy to be here, Sam," Diana said into her microphone.

"So, we've run down most of the story as we knew it. But we've learned so much since then. But first, I wanted to let everyone know we are also joined by a few special guests, and it's time to meet the man, the myth, the legend behind our cameras. DeMarcus Jackson. "

DeMarcus had set the camera up on a gimbal that tracked voices so he could join the podcast round table.

"I am also happy to be here, Sam," He said with an excited grin.

"How's the recovery been?" Diana asked.

"Great, we had a great team of doctors and nurses at the hospital, so I'm basically back to normal."

"That's great." She smiled warmly at him.

"So the question we get asked the most in the comment section that our viewers want to know is, when did you realize Brent was the bad guy in all of this? Were there any signs, looking back, that you wish you had noticed sooner?" Sam said, kicking off the questions.

"For me, it was that moment in the parking lot of the diner," Diana responded. That she had thought of him as a bulldozer with a sweet teddy bear persona inside was now disgusting to her. Maybe it was because he had reminded her of her dad. But it had really hurt her feelings and her pride that she didn't clock him sooner.

"Yeah... I mean, the guy was a little weird. I spent more time with him than you guys, but I mean, aren't all men in their 50's a little weird?" DeMarcus added.

"Weird how?" Sam asked.

"Well, for one, his story about his wife leaving him and taking his kids... there were no photos of his kids on his phone. Hell, there were no photos on his phone. At the time, I thought maybe he just wasn't into technology, but he did all the editing for the episode, so now looking back, that was weird."

"That's a great point, yeah, we've been able to confirm. He's never been married and doesn't have any known kids."

"Thank God...could you imagine finding out that piece of shit was your dad?" Diana added.

Sam ignored that, but gripped her hand under the table. Diana could feel the look she knew he wanted to give her. Teasing him with off-the-wall comments was one of her favorite pastimes.

"Yeah, now looking back at it, and I'm not sure how much of this you saw, Diana, but there was always stuff going wrong on this case. Battery packs not being charged for the cameras, sections of film being deleted, the flat tires, missed appointments, hell, even the Airbnb we stayed at was a last-minute thing I booked while you were sleeping on the plane after our hotel fell through."

"Really...I never knew. I figured you got the house on purpose." She said.

"It was an idea I'd had after meeting you, but the hotel was already supposedly booked. I went to cancel it to get the house and found out the reservation never existed."

"Do you want to tell the viewers why you had that idea?" DeMarcus added with a sly grin..

Sam gave him a look.

"Well. We had witnessed a public fight in our hotel lobby when we were checking out. And after experiencing Diana's temper that first time we met... I just felt like it would be a better environment for Diana."

"AWWW, that was so thoughtful," Diana said with a warm squeeze of her hand under the table.

"We made the most of it, but yeah. There were several red flags we should have paid more attention to. "

"So what's happened to Brent/ Keith now?" Diana asked. She knew the answer, but felt like it was a helpful question to move the pace along into the episode.

"Well, he's still in jail. He didn't get bond. The grand jury was brought in because there's gonna be a lot of investigations started because of this case." Sam responded.

"Like the man in the picture? Have they identified him yet?" She asked.

"Yes, actually, we did," Sam told her.

"When we actually started looking into him. It involved a lot of grunt work. But it occurred to me to basically start a web of influence around Reagan, her mom, Brent, her manager...anyone that had control in her life, basically. Then go and look for known associates. Cross-reference that list with known sex offenders, because it seemed likely that the man was probably a repeat offender, and it turns out I was right."

"Really?" Diana was surprised.

"Yeah, it was the manager's brother-in-law," Sam said.

Diana stared back in shock.

"He was arrested immediately after the grand jury yesterday, so I wanted to tell you. You don't have to worry about him anymore."

"That is awesome to hear."

"Yes, the guys at LAPD are really coming through, and actually, let me bring him up on the screen here, your friend Pete wanted to drop by and say Hi," Sam said with a smile, holding up a tablet with Pete on video chat.

"Oh my god, Hi Pete!" Diana squealed.

"Hi, Diana. Hey guys." Pete said from the tablet.

"We are so glad you could make it," Sam said, pulling the tablet back to face himself.

"We've got news to share," Sam said, barely containing his glee.

"Really?" Pete asked

"We're engaged! He said, holding up Diana's hand.

"Congratulations," Pete said, and DeMarcus gave a small golf clap but was grinning from ear to ear.

"So, are you gonna talk about that?" DeMarcus asked, pointing between the two of them.

"Well, when a smart, feisty, beautiful woman walks into your life, you don't question much, you just try to keep up," Sam said with a grin, pulling her hand up to his mouth to brush a kiss over the back of her knuckles in a sweet gesture.

"Feisty is definitely one word for her...hey Pete, you had something you wanted to share?" DeMarcus asked.

"Yeah... obviously with the police investigation and this now going to trial, there's a lot I can't share, but I did want to tell you we identified the person on the motorcycle who was following you that one day."

"Really, who?" Diana asked.

"Harry Jepsen, actually. We were able to place his phone there at the same time as you guys."

"Really?" Sam was also surprised.

"Yeah, so this whole thing with him and Brent, it was orchestrated a lot more than we thought," Pete added.

"I guess so. You know it's funny. It was his idea to invite Diana to join us in L.A.." Sam told them.

"Really? Now, why would he do that?" She wondered.

"Maybe he always wanted to kill you? Because you were the last thing standing between him and freedom, as the only person who would want to push to have the case re-investigated." Pete speculated.

"Maybe, or maybe, he knew Sam's type and figured she would be a good distraction. We were all too busy wondering, will they or won't they? We never noticed how much sabotage was going on," DeMarcus said.

"What got sabotaged?" Diana asked.

"Like all the filming after episode one got deleted. I only saved that by thinking to back it up myself." DeMarcus told her.

"Yep, so we were able to show a lot of our time in L.A., but not the trip to Oregon, where Diana punched a tree, or the phone call with Reagan's teacher, Linda, or her friend Tuyet. But we did get this clip I wanted to share today..."

Sam looked at her with a sly smile.

"Yeah.. shout-out to Linda and Tuyet, y'all were game changers on helping us solve this case," Diana said quickly as a TV behind them came on, and their car ride to Dunsmuir started playing. It was when she told Sam about her gator incident.

They were all cracking up by the end of it.

"Sounds like you're gonna have your hands full, Sam..." Pete said.

"Yeah, and I'm gonna love every minute of it."

The End

Reviews

I sincerely hope you have enjoyed this story. It would mean the world to me to have you share your thoughts. I have linked the various review websites on my website for your convenience.

ravenrisingbooks.wordpress.com/reviews/

About the Author

Raven is a Carolina native who's called both North and South Carolina home. She holds a Master's degree in Administration of Justice with a concentration in Criminal Behavior and brings firsthand experience as a former 911 dispatcher and certified firearms instructor.

A passionate reader and true crime podcast enthusiast, Raven blends her love of storytelling with her background in public safety to create realistic, emotionally gripping thrillers. When she's not writing, she works full-time in a firearm-related industry, where she advocates for gun rights, personal responsibility, and empowering others to become their own first responder.

She lives with her husband and their two adorably chaotic cats, and is always working on her next great story.

You can connect with me on:

🌐 https://ravenrisingbooks.com
f https://www.facebook.com/people/Raven-Rising-Books/61577621337215
🔗 https://www.tiktok.com/@authorravenlynne

Also by Raven Lynne

Under pen name Raven Conces a new story emerges... Coming 2026

Rising Crime

Book 1 of the Rising Calls Series

When a series of home invasions strikes close to home, 911 dispatcher **Cassie Bennett** finds herself navigating both the chaos on the radio and the fear gripping her own neighborhood. As the lines blur between the calls she takes and the people she knows. Cassie will have to use every skill she's learned and trust her instincts like never before to survive what's coming.